The Release

The Release

S.M. GOLD

AuthorHouse™
1663 Liberty Drive
Bloomington, IN 47403
www.authorhouse.com
Phone: 1 (800) 839-8640

Published by AuthorHouse 05/19/2015

ISBN: 978-1-5049-1286-0 (sc)
ISBN: 978-1-5049-1285-3 (e)

Print information available on the last page.

Any people depicted in stock imagery provided by Thinkstock are models, and such images are being used for illustrative purposes only.
Certain stock imagery © Thinkstock.

This book is printed on acid-free paper.

Because of the dynamic nature of the Internet, any web addresses or links contained in this book may have changed since publication and may no longer be valid. The views expressed in this work are solely those of the author and do not necessarily reflect the views of the publisher, and the publisher hereby disclaims any responsibility for them.

It was a cold day as I awoke to go to the office. Just another day of taking shit from people there and wondering if I am ever going to find happiness in my life, the day seemed to go on forever finally it was lunch and I went to the dinner up the street and ordered my usual ham on rye and a coffee like I needed more caffeine.

I picked up my book and started to read and thought, I wish this would happen to me, be swept off my feet and controlled, then I thought to myself who am I kidding, me controlled not going to happen it's a romance novel they all have happy endings and I can't even find a happy start. This is just a book, well so I thought.

Across the dinner was a terribly handsome man sitting there going over some documents he had a strange look on his face. He glanced up and had an evil grin on his face but at the same time he looked serious I was wondering what he was thinking about. He was very mysterious just like the man in my book, just he was better looking and dressed much nicer.

Time had flown by and wow I was late to go back to work I gathered my things and jumped up and almost ran for the door. I ran right into him. He had a cup of coffee and it spilled all over him oh my god I'm sorry I'll clean that for you he smiled and said I didn't mean to embarrass you by calling you that but I don't know your name. She bent her head down and turned even redder and said my name is Julie I work across the street and with that I left.

A few days later she was at a restaurant with some girlfriends from work and a waiter came over with a bottle of wine and four glasses and said the gentlemen at the end of the bar sent it over. She told him to send it back thank you we were just leaving. He did as she requested and sent it back. Her and her friend got up to leave and once again she ran into him he smiled and said nice to see you without you head in a book Julie. She smiled and said thank you but we're in a hurry and once again left without saying anything else.

Her friends asked who was that he is fricking cute. Julie turned red again because she also thought he was cute, but didn't want him to know well not yet at least. Julie said someone I met at the dinner I'm so clumsy I spilt his coffee on his shirt. I guess I should have thanked him for the drink, oh will maybe another time...

Mike saw her coming and stood up as she approached and asked if she would like to sit for a minute? She said well maybe for a minute I'm already late for work. Mike pulled a chair out for her and then sat back down. I'm so glad you decided to sit for a minute. I so wanted to get your number the other day but once again you were in such a hurry.

So what do you do if I may ask? Julie said a little of everything, mainly I answer the phones make copies for everyone but I like to stay busy. I don't like to sit still much it drives me nuts. He smiled at her and said yes you seem like you have pent up energy, but I bet I could help you with that and help you learn some self-control.

Oh really she said jokingly, Mike said yes really you have no idea the things I like to do for play and by the way I went and bought a copy of the book you were reading. I wanted to see why you were so red and what was keeping you so focused. Your book likes talking about control a lot, they have no idea what control is my house keeper cold control someone better than he could.

Julie was now embarrassed, oh shit, I was reading a smut book and now this very handsome man knows and thinks I'm a slut or something. She cleared her throat and said, I need to get back to my friends now and stood up. Mike stood up and grabbed her hand and said I didn't mean to embarrass you I was actually trying to put you at rest a little, can I give you my number before you run off? I would like to talk with you may be over lunch unless you will let me take you out for diner just once, he reached in his pocket and pulled out a card. On it read was his name and phone number and it said lifestyle couch. She took the card, said thank you and went back to her friends.

He watched as her and her friend went and danced with each other, and with men sometimes she looked so hot in that tight dress. He knew she had gone home and changed because that wasn't office wear at all. It was about 11p.m., now mike had a busy day. Julie hadn't realized he had left. She had been watching him out the corner of her eye while she was dancing, trying to look very sensual to him.

When she got back to the table she wasn't in such a girly mood anymore, in fact she told her friends it was getting late, so she was going to call it a night. They said ok we will see you tomorrow at work. She lived four blocks away so she walked, it wasn't quite this cold when she got there.

She closed her coat and started to walk at a very fast pace trying to keep warn it wasn't easy in stilettos, though about half a block up the road a limo pulled over and the rear window went down a gentleman's voice said from the inside of the car, Julie you poor thing you will freeze to death get in. This shocked her, she didn't know anyone with a limp so she looked in a little closer. It was Mike. She smiled and said, oh I just live about three blocks up he said its ok I'll give you a lift. Reluctantly, she said yes, she was so very cold in this dress.

The driver got out and opened the door for her. She sat on the same seat but at the other end as he was. He said I didn't mean to scare you, but you did look very cold. Julie said thank you I was. Mike said by the comment I made about control in the book I'm sorry I hate authors that think they know about the lifestyle but don't except what they have read. It really isn't like that, there are a few parts that are real, but for the most part the book is wrong.

Julie said oh with disappointment, she liked the book and had dreamed it could be her in that position. Mike said if you're interested in learning about the lifestyle I would love to tell you about it and maybe if you like even show you. She made a gulping sound ummmm well I would like to hear more about it but I don't think I'd ever be able to do any of it. I get embarrassed way to easy.

Mike said well one never knows till they try. Most people find things very enjoyable and relaxing. About then she spoke up and said that's my place on the right driver, so the driver pulled over and got out to let her out, but waited until he was instructed to do so. Julie said it was nice talking with you and thank you so much for the ride. Mike said glad to help, he motioned the driver to open the door as she was getting out, and Julie leaned over and said if you are sure you wouldn't mind telling me more I'd love to know more.

Mike smiled because he knew he got her interested just enough to keep her wanting to know more. He said sure no problem call me tomorrow and I'll pick you up after work and we can go to dinner. Julie said ok, that would be great, thanks again and walked into her apt. building.

It really wasn't in a good part of town and mike wondered if the beautiful young lady would be ok, he had other things in mind for her, he had this knack of reading people, knowing just what they were hiding, and just that they needed. A trick he had learned long ago from a job he had in the past.

When he got home he couldn't get her off his mind there was just something about her. He was going to make his no matter what. He went to sleep smiling and dreaming of her with his collar on. When Julie got into her apt. she undressed, it was getting late. She needed to get to sleep, she had to work in the morning. She laid there but she couldn't stop thinking about him or what his card said, lifestyle couch. She wondered what it meant seeing how he said what he did about the book. It was like he knew so much more about it than the author did.

She really liked the book and couldn't imagine anything better than that. He finally drifted off to sleep and in the morning woke up and still thinking about Mike wow! Was he really interested in her? All she could think of is I hope so. She got ready and went to work and at lunch as always went to the diner across the street. As she walked in there he sat. Julie come sit with me, I've already ordered your lunch. Julie smiled. Wow! He must have asked them what I liked or something.

She sat down and again said thank you, he said you don't have to be so surprised. She said, well it's not like that, I like the fact that you ordered my lunch I don't know why no one has never don't that but I like it. Mike smiled and said I enjoy taking control of things that's why I'm a real Dom not like the one in that book you have been reading.

Julie's eyes widened and said, really with a little bit of fear I think in her voice Mike spoke up and said I'm sorry I didn't mean to scare you. It's just I like being up front and blunt about things, Julie said, no you didn't scare me just surprised me. I think, wow. So tell me more in the book they were talking about these different girls I think they were called slaves and subs, can you tell me about it because, it actually interested me very much, but I didn't think there were such things as a Dom or Sub.

Mike smiled and said I would love to but that would take a while how about we talk about that over drinks and dinner tonight. I'll pick you up at 6. This way we can swing by your place so you can change and we will have several hours to talk about it ok. Julie said, ok, great. I would love to learn more, but for now I better get back to work.

Mike spent the day trying to figure out how to explain things to her without scaring her off. Hummm, I have it, he picked up his phone and called someone he knew named, Carl and told him what was going on and asked if he could borrow his sub, thinking it might help ease things this evening Carl said, well how about Lisa and I both come this way she can see firsthand when you're ready of course we will sit at a different table until then. Mike said ok great that will work.

Mike was there at six o'clock sharp to pick her up. They drove back to her place, he started to get out with her, she said would you mind waiting in the car my apt. is kind of small and my roommates are home. I live with two other females. Mike smiled and said ok no problem. She returned in just a few minutes, she was dressed to kill, in her little black, WOW! It showed off every curve she had.

When they got to the restaurant Carl and Lisa, were already there. Mike had called and reserved tow tables side by side. Mike pulled the chair out for Julie, they sat down, and he ordered a bottle of wine. Mike looked at her and said you look lovely tonight Julie said thank you as do you Mike.

He smiled a little, so you would like to learn more about the lifestyle, subs, slaves and Dom's. Julie lit up and said yes I would if you don't mind. Mike said I don't mind at all. Julie's eyes kept wondering to the table next to ours where Carl and his sub, Lisa sat. She was dressed very nice and had a black leather collar on. She was watching closely to her body, about then Carl slapped her hand and said, I said you have had enough for now, the girl lowered her head and said yes Sir sorry Sir.

Mike had been talking to her about the role of the Dom, which is to nourish, guide, protect, and that the Dom always watches out for his sub, or slave. In return the sub or slave does as she is told at all times without question and without hesitation. About then Julie spoke up and said wow that was man was rude to her. Mike smiled and said well whatever happened I'm sure it was in her best interest. Julie said yea just like a man. Mikes face got serious, oh really let's see about that.

Mike turned and motioned for the couple from the table to join us. Julie was embarrassed and said you don't have to do this, Mike said yes I do. Carl and Lisa came over, Mike said please sit down. Julie was confused. Julie let me introduce you to a friend of in this is Carl, and this is his sup Lisa.

THE RELEASE

Julie was livid now oh gawd, this was embarrassing. Nice to meet you. Mike spoke up and said Carl why were you disciplining Lisa a few minutes ago. Julie thought you were being rude to her. Carl said oh, heavens no she had already had two glasses of wine and was after drinking another and grabbed the glass after I had said no.

Julie spoke up and said will she is a grown adult, Carl said yes she is but she is my sub and will do as I say or will be punished. I am looking out for her best interest if she has another glass so soon she will get sick and my dear we are in a restaurant and that wouldn't be good. About then Lisa spoke up and said I'm ok he is right I tend to get carried away and I'm very glad he looks out for me so well, that is why I love him. Julie smiled and said wow. I was way off I'm so sorry. Carl said its fine things aren't always as they appear.

Mike spoke up and said see I told you there was an explanation for it... So would you still like to learn? Julie said yes can I ask what that leather is around your neck Lisa. Lisa looked at Carl and asked if she could speak openly and freely with her. Carl said by all means you may. So the girls scooted closer to each other and began to talk. Julie seemed more and more excited with the whole concept of it all.

Mike was pleased with everything that had happened this evening, even with Lisa getting in trouble. After a little bit Carl said well we need to Say our good nights to you, its late and I still want to get a play session in with my sub before I retire for the night. Mike said ok I will talk to you tomorrow, thanks for allowing Lisa to talk with her.

When they left Julie had a funny look on her face, she was in awe over it all, and she really wanted what Lisa had but didn't know how she could get it. Mike, after a few seconds said is something wrong? Julie said no not at all just the opposite very right actually. Mike said what, you will have to explain that one, sorry. Julie realized what she had said and was now a pretty pink color, Mike said no need to be embarrassed I think I already know what you're going to say, but I'd like to hear it from you, please Julie lowered her head and began to mumble something he couldn't understand. Mike said Julie stop this and just tell me in a very strict voice and without even realizing she said sorry sir, and began to tell him that she would like to try being a sub.

Mike said well there is a lot to it, I would be happy to teach you and train you and at the end of it I would be happy to have you as my sub… Julie's face lit up really thank you, are you sure, I mean I've never done anything like this but it fascinates me so much, I would just love to, Mike stopped her in mid word. Julie stop she did as she was told and again said sorry sir, Mike smiled and said good girl you learn fast. Julie just smiled.

Mike stood up and said well now its late and you have to work tomorrow correct, Julie said no I have tomorrow off, Mike smiled a funny little smile and said really well then would you like to come to my place, I have a guest bedroom and I can show you my play room. You will have lots of questions when you see it, but this is what Carl was also talking about when he said play time with Lisa.

Julie said well I'm not sure, are you sure it's ok? Mike said yes, I have a large home all to myself except first thing in the morning and at meal times, I have a lady that comes in and cooks and cleans but she doesn't stay there with me. Julie said well ok, if you're sure. So they got up and drove back to his house well that is what he called it.

I called it a mansion, WOW! It was huge. We walked in. Julie was in awe with it. She had never seen such a place before he gave her a tour and they stopped at a door and said this is my play room, but right now I don't have a sub. I am currently seeking one. Julie smiled and said well now you never know Mike said no you don't.

He opened the door and there were all these things, there was wood shaped like an x with cuffs on it and all sorts of things. She had never seen before oh my she said mike said no it's not like you think a lot of females enjoy a small amount of pain, it gives them a lot of pleasure and release as I enjoy them enjoying themselves as well. Julie said oh ok. That makes sense I will have to try some of these.

Mike said in time, how about we start simple. Do you know what these are? Julie turned red and said well of course there vibrators. Mike spoke up and said excuse me this you will learn to stop. Sorry sir, yes Sir. I know what they are and he picked up another and said and this Julie said, yes sir it's called a butt plug I tried that once but never had the chance again. Will then he said you will have that chance again they talked for hours and Julie got more and more excited about the whole thing, could this all be real, seriously.

The next morning they continued talking. She had a few days off and really enjoyed talking to him and found more out. It was Tuesday night and mike said how about we try some things out. Tomorrow we will go out for dinner and take things from there. Seeing that Julie was falling into place very nicely. Julie said ok in the morning he was showing her things in his play room and asked if he would try some different things on her. Mike said well if you are sure I'd love to see how you react to some of these, Julie smiled.

Mike said well first off get undressed, Julie said ok being the eager beaver she was, she did love to please people and now, what Sir Mike said sit here in the middle of the room on your haunches and do not look a t me unless told, understand. Julie said yes Sir. She moved where he had told her and waited.

Then he said come here she did as told again. Mike smiled and said good girl. There was something about that being said that put her even more at ease with everything he said now, seeing how you said you knew what all these were, let's see if that's the truth. Julie said, but I've never had anyone else use them on me I mean, Mike spoke sharply as I said let's see, lay down on the bed and your hands above your head and spread your feet apart. Julie did as she was told.

Mike walked over and began to cuff her to the bed. She hesitated for a second that is your only warning you will not hesitate when told to do something understand. Julie said yes sir sorry sir he finished restraining her hands and feet and then started to use the vibrator on her clit she clenched her teeth.

Mike said oh no baby girl open your mouth and breath, I want to hear you, but sir no I can't mike stopped what he was doing and reached over and got a crop and slapped thigh, with oh shit, she yelled, you son of a bitch. Mike slammed it down again and excuse me you were told do not question, do not hesitate, Julie lowered her eyes and said yes sir sorry sir.

Mike again started with the vibrators and Julie's body began to shake, oh gawd, Sir I'm Cuming please stop please sir. Mike didn't stop, instead he grabbed another and inserted it inside her. She let out a scream that could be heard threw out the house of ecstasy.

Mike wasn't done. Julie didn't know what to think, she had never came so hard before and never more than once she was so sensitive. Mike said well now let's try this baby girl you will have to relax for this a minute. Julie didn't know what he was doing, but right then didn't care.

Mike grabbed a butt plug, put lube on it and started to insert it. Julie yelped a little but let him continue. She didn't want the crop again he then put the vibrator back on her clit again and began to move it around. Julie was feeling things she never had before, her body began to shake she clenched her teeth, Mike stopped. Julie caught her breath and said why did you stop?

Mike said because I told you to keep your mouth open, you didn't so for now we're done we will continue after dinner. Julie was saddened by this she was so turned on right now she couldn't stand it. Mike untied her and helped her up so what do you think so far baby girl. Julie smiled and said wow I really enjoyed that a lot.

Mike said oh it only gets better trust me. She started to get dressed and realized she had the butt plug still in. She said excuse me sir may I go to the bathroom and pull this out. Mike smiled and said no leave it in till after dinner. Julie said you're crazy and headed for the bathroom, turn around Mike ordered she wasn't listening to him it wasn't a request she stopped and turned around what did I say earlier you do as you are told. He got his crop again and this time he laid it across her ass when will you learn to listen, I do hate doing this.

4

N ow go and get dressed and put some makeup on so we can go eat, I'm hungry he said. She was just taking her time messing about in the room still and then Mike spoke up again.

It wasn't a request.

A simple Wednesday night out at our favorite diner, except tonight I'd be filled with a large plug up in my ass, with my clit resting against a remote controlled vibrator tucked perfectly in my lace panties, and yes, he'd be bolding the remote control all evening.

Turn around he said again, a slight look of surprise at my hesitation crossing his handsome face.

I did as I was told and was rewarded with his hand caressing my back before he firmly pushed me face down on the bed pulling up my short black skirt and dragging my panties down past my knees. The soft click of the lube bottle next to the bed made my breathing hitch a moment. I'd seen this plug once before. It was quite large; a red, diamond-shaped cone with a wide base. Wouldn't want it slipping out, they had told me once with a grin not too long ago.

A strong hand began kneading my left cheek, and I heard him murmur a soft approval as the fingers of his other hand, slick with lubrication, started rubbing my sensitive hole he gently slipped on finger, then two, continually kneading and caressing me. A moment later I felt the push of the plug.

Relax, baby, he whispered. I took a deep breath and exhaled. The plug moved deeper into my ass as his fingers started circling my clit. I could feel myself getting wet for him, and couldn't help pushing my hips off the bed to meet his hand, his soft chuckle made me blush.

Does that feel good, little girl?

God yes. It did.

Almost there, he said. There was just a second of burning, but I was too distracted by his fingers on my clit to care. The moment the plug was all the way in and I felt that blissful feeling of fullness, I started to cum.

A quick slap on my ass brought me back to the moment as he hauled me up to my feet and told me to pull my panties back up. When I finally turned around to face him, he pulled me close and settled a small almost flat vibrator into the base of my black lace panties. It fit perfectly against my pussy, and I could feel a small bump that rested next to my now quite swollen clit.

There, he said stepping back to admire his handiwork. All ready for dinner don't you look nice. I had taken care in getting ready for him this evening. Of course I'd be wearing a short skirt and heels. I added a form fitting black top. He'd made another request that night for a pretty necklace and earrings. To look all dressed up, even when I was naked, as he had put it, I liked that idea. But, then again, I would dress however he'd ask me to. I love to see the look of approval on his face when he first sees me.

As I smoothed down my skirt and he helped me into my coat, I couldn't help but wonder how I was even going to walk, let alone make it through an entire evening meal. As if sensing my thoughts, he gave me a smile as we stepped out of his apartment and I felt a sudden pulsing against my pussy. It made me jump and yelp in surprise. His blue eyes flashed with amusement and started to laugh.

Oh, this was going to be fun, the said tucking the remote in his jacket pocket. The ride to the diner downtown was equal parts fun and frustration. As much as he usually to watch me cum, tonight it appeared, he wanted to watch me almost cum; at least until he was ready to let me cum. Between turning the vibrator on and off at varying intervals, any bump on the street pushed on the plug and made me squeeze my thighs together.

The closer to orgasm I'd get the firmer his tough would become on my thigh. His hand felt so strong and warm on my skin. I love how he grabs my inner thigh and gives me an occasional squeeze. That drives me crazy. He gave me a clear warning as we parked that I had to wait to cum, and then made it even more difficult for me with a deep kiss that made my skin tingle all over.

God I love the way he kisses me.

Every step from the car to the restaurant was torture as the fullness of the plug and the pressure of the vibrator had me so sensitive; I felt that I could orgasm right there on the sidewalk. It didn't help that once we got into the diner all the benches were make of hard wood. No matter how I sat- upright, to the side, or with my pelvis tucked under, the nub of the vibrator pushed against my swollen clit, and the base of the plug drove deeper into my ass.

I couldn't concentrate on the menu, and just ordered my usual. When I glanced up at his face it seemed he was studying me. What? I asked, unable to contain my curiosity anymore, I always had trouble reading his thoughts, but this was a thousand times worse as I was being driven to distraction sitting on that hard seat.

I was just deciding if I wanted you to cum right here or not, he said with a slight furrowed brow, the look of serious contemplation quickly was replaced with a wicked flash of heat in his amazing sea-blue eyes.

A look like that alone from him is often enough to make me wet. With all the sensations I was feeling at the moment, I would gladly have cum, and loudly, in front of everyone in the room if he'd asked me to. He reached into his jacket for the remote, and even though I knew what to expect, I couldn't help but jump as the vibration started.

My hips rocked involuntarily, and within moments I was starting to get hot and close to the edge. The room around me didn't matter. I could care less who was looking, or who might guess what was happening to me. I closed my eyes and started to let go…, and then it all stopped.

Opening my eyes, I found him looking at me with a quite smile. No, I decided you're not going to cum here after all, he said and with that he started enjoying his dinner/ all I could do was stare back at him in a bit of disbelief, and try to regain a normal rhythm of breathing.

I hardly remember eating. I don't remember really what we talked about, and who knows how long we sat there. It seemed like an eternity to me. When we finally got up to go, my legs were so shaky. I swear if he had turned that little gadget, I would have crumpled to the floor. It took every bit of my concentration to steadily walk the two city blocks back to the car. It didn't help to look up at him. Walking next me, holding my hand. So tall, so sexy. I could feel myself getting wet every time he would glance down at me as we strolled.

You ok, little girl? He asked, halfway down the second block. I nodded and squeezed his hand. Without waiting he turned and pinned me against the smooth stone of the building next to us. I loved feeling the length of his body against mine, and when the vibrator started, the held me tightly as I started to squirm. His strong hand found my throat and gripped my jaw as he kissed me, smoothly dancing his tongue with mine I could barely catch my breath as he moved his mouth to my ear and began to kiss me there.

I'm going to fuck you and make you scream, he whispered, making my knees buckle. I felt my orgasm build, my hips starting to press against the outline of his hard cock in his jeans. So close, just a moment more... oh please let me cum this time... And then it stopped. Fuck.

He pulled back, grabbed my hand, smiled at me and started whaling once more. I must have walked back to the car with him. I honestly don't remember. Sitting next to him on the smooth cushions of the car didn't bring any relief, however. He had something more in mind. With another devilish smile he produced from his pocket a pair of tweezer nipple clamps complete with a heavy connecting chain.

I thought these might have been a bit much for dinner, he said reaching over to me and gently pulling down my V-neck top. He carefully rolled one nipple between his finger and thumb until it stood at attention for him. Watching my face, the tightened the clamp until. I gasped from the sharp sting. He replaced the torment on the other breast, finishing with a gentle flick of his thumb on each nipple.

Now we can go home, he said, and started the engine.

As I pulled away from the curb I smiled. She always gave me such pleasure. The night had been one to remember so far. She had turned into such an anal slut and I had to admit that I enjoyed it. Her ass was nice and tight. I always enjoyed fucking it. When I had shown her the anal plug she had gotten tense but it wasn't long until she had asked me to use it on her.

Now I knew she enjoyed her anal torment.

Glancing over I could see her hard nipples pressing tightly against her blouse as the street lights strobes through the car. She was certainly a very, very attractive woman and I enjoyed others admiring her. Tonight she had dressed so elegantly knowing that she was pleasing me. She was an exhibitionist. She got a huge turn-on knowing men or women were looking at her.

Now driving home the bumps in the road were driving her closer and closer to cumin. She knew she couldn't without my permission. Still the nipple clamps, the butt plug and the vibrator were pushing her closer and closer. Please Sir, make me cum for you.

Stopping at the light I leaned towards her, reaching my arm around and pulling her lips to mine. I kissed her passionately while my hand reached over and pinched her tingling nipples hard. She cried out into my lips please sir. Make me cum for you.

Reaching for the chain I take it in my hand and tug at it. This brings a shriek from her oh my gawd Sir I keep tugging on the chain as I whisper in her "cum for me baby girl. Show me what a hot slut you are". This causes her to suddenly release all the passion that had been building all night. Her body starts shaking as her hips begin grinding up and sown as if she were riding a nice big cock. Her mouth was open and a low growl was coming from deep within her.

Then it hit her skirt had riding up until I could see her wet panties and now she was cumin and soaking them even more. Gawd I loved it when she couldn't control herself and she squirted when she came. She always tried to hide it but it came out once when I had her tied and was pushing her further and further until when she came, she squirted all down her thighs.

Ever since, I always push her until she squirted her juices for me. Now she was slumped down in the seat breathing deeply. Her eyes glazed over with such a fierce lust that I knew the night was still young. She had grown into one of his most favorite pets. The light changes and he turned his attention back to the road. They drove on into the night listening to my music selection. As we pulled up to the house I parked and shut down the car.

Looking over at her I reached out and tugged again on the chain connected to the clips. This brought a groan from her as she turned to him panting, Sir are you coming in with me. I knew what she was asking and she was in for a surprise. I had arranged with her husband to show him what a good pet she was.

He wanted to see her controlled and take the way he couldn't. In the past, I have never entered into her house. I had kept our relationship between us. However she had come to me, asking that I write to her husband because he wanted to ask me something. She had no idea what it was. She cared for her husband but there wasn't that part that made it a lasting relationship. She knew deep in her heart that she loved her master. That she would do whatever I wanted just so I would be pleased.

I turned the vibrator down and got out of the car. I walked around and opened her door. She looked up into my eyes as I reached out and took her hand. Let's go inside. Her eyes widened with shock as she stood on eh shaking legs saying yes Sir we walked up the side walk and steps to her front door. She struggled to get her keys out as she was still in shock.

What was going to happen? Had her husband and him set something up for tonight? Whatever it was, she wasn't going to let anything ruin this moment. She opened the door and stood back saying please come in Sir. I stepped in and looked around she had told me so much about her house and now is was seeing it for the first time. Honey is that you? Came from the kitchen as she nervously looked towards the door and back to me. Yes it is. Is your master with you?

Looking into my eyes she says yes he is, why don't you come into the den and introduce us. I smile and follow her through the house. We reach the den and she stands to my side. I step forward and introduce myself and shake his hand. Then I turn, reach my arm out and around her waist pulling her to me. With my other hand, I reach up and tug the chain holding the clips on her nipples. She groans oh gawd Sir. Then turning to her husband, I reach into my pocket and turn the vibrator on high as I look into his eyes.

She crumples against me as her body gives ways. He asks can I watch no I say he looks sown and says ok I've moved my stuff in the guest room and I will say good night. She looked up as he walked by saying goodnight. I tugged hard on the chain causing her to moan, Sir yes Sir. I moved to the couch and sit down. Put on some music and dance for me. Yes Sir.

I sat back as she went to their stereo and cut it on. She picked out a hot cd and pushed play. The music filled the room and she began moving to the music. It had been a while sense I clipped her nipples so I motioned her to me. She seductively moved to me. I indicated for her to near and she obeyed. I then brushed her blouse aside and tugged at the chain tying her stiff nipples together. She threw her head back wanting to scream but held it in. I loved it. She could handle such pain and would never give a whimper. Actually it would often be much the opposite.

She usually would cum screaming her release. I held out my hand. She looked back down at my hand and slowly leaned forward. Placing a tender, sensitive nipple in it. I pinched the tinder tip and she bit her lip. Then I release the clip. The blood rush into her nipples causes her to give a squeal. I then roll the beautiful nipple between my fingers allowing the blood to engorge it and watch as it swells. Her eyes are closed and her hands trembling as she holds my arm.

I then hold my other hand out. She leans forward and places the other gorgeous tit in it. Once again I pinch the tender tip and release the clip. She can hardly control herself as she wants to pull away from my fingers. I roll the nipple between my fingers and tug at it watching as it swells.

She knows what to do next and slowly raises and moves forward. I sit back as she straddles my lap and feeds me one of her very excited nipples. My warm lips and hot tongue caress it roughly as she groan Sir my gawd Sir. I suck sucked hard on the sensitive nipple and bite at its tip then noisily pop it from my lips. She then turns and feeds me the other nipple. I treat it the same as the other with the exception of reaching around as I suck on her nipple and push her butt plug against her ass. She screams oh gawd sir may I please cum. "No"

I say as I release her torrid nipple and tell her to dance for me now.

Slopping from my lap she glances and sees the bulge in my trousers. She always likes to excite and please me. Standing on shaky legs she moves to the center of the room and begins moving slowly to the music. I sit back and reach down stroking my hard cock watching her show. Moving so seductively she enjoys these moments. It's her time to control the situation and she knows exactly what she is doing.

Slowly unbuttoning her blouse she slips it from her shoulders letting it drop to the floor. She looks gorgeous. Her big tits shake and juggle as she dances. She knows I love them and she flaunts them for me. Reaching and squeezing them as her nipples swell even more. The slightest touch of her nipples will set her off and she is careful to avoid them.

A slow song comes on and she holds her hands out to me. I smile calling her husband back to the room. She looks puzzled as he comes back in looking from me to his topless wife dancing for this stranger. "What's going on here" he ask. "She needs someone to dance with" and I point to her.

Turning to his wife his eyes widen as he sees her tits and nipples. They are so swollen and hard. She knows not to question me and reaches for him. "Come dance with me baby" she calls. He can't stop himself. It's been so long since she has allowed him to touch her. Seeing her like this has his blood boiling with lust. He didn't care that there was a stranger watching them. He moved forward and took her into his arms. She groaned trying to pull away from him as her nipples brushed his shirt.

I smile knowing she could cum so easily. I wouldn't let that happen just yet. I wanted her to squirt like she never had this time. Holding him close she began dancing seductively. She was looking over his shoulder watching me as he held her close and reached down to squeeze her ass. As he did, her eyes shot wide and her body pressed tighter to him as her hands shot down to push his hands away.

Then moving away from him she moved to the table and pulled out a chair. She then told him "sit down baby and let me give you a lap dance". He couldn't believe it. He had asked her to do this many times and she never would. He had herd she had once danced and had a reputation of being extremely good. Now he was going to experience it firsthand.

Sitting down he looked over to me. I smiled saying "she is very good isn't she". He looked back to his wife and then back to me saying "oh gawd yes". She then dropped her skirt leaving her in heels, nylons and panties. Gawd she looked good. I had to admit that if I wasn't carful things could get awful complicated with us. I made my mind up then and watched the show.

She moved over and began giving her husband a dance he would never forget. She straddled his leg at one point and almost lost it. As she grinned down at him, the plug in her ass was pushed deeper. I remembered the vibrator in my pocket and pushed it up high. This caused her to lose her balance and she ended up against him. He took it as her excitement and took a stiff nipple between his excited lips.

She cussed "oh gawd damn you, no", and pulled away from him. He looked like someone had just took his lollipop away from him.

She kept dancing and bent down to him saying, "No toughing baby, I'm not your play toy, I am my masters". She then turned towards me, spread her legs and slowly squatted showing me her soaked panties. Running her hands up her long thighs until they reached her panties.

Then looking into my eyes, she pushed them aside to show me her open swollen pussy. I could see her lips swollen and open, they were wet and like a flower petals spread revealing that delicious pussy. I wanted to jump up and attack her and it took all my will power to sit back stroking my hard cock. Pre cum had already started dripping from the head and she noticed the big wet spot forming on my trousers leg. Smiling she released her panties and slowly stood back up. She began dancing again towards her husband. I knew the butt plug was keeping her from putting on the show she could do.

"Let him take your plug out". She turned quickly to me and pleaded with her eyes, "are you sure Sir". I didn't like to be questioned and put my legs together telling her, get over "here and bend across my lap". She realized what she had done and slowly moved to me. Carefully laying across my lap she stuck her sweet ass up in the air. "I misbehaved and need to be punished Sir". My hand moved quickly and I slapped her ass hard. She didn't dare move as she bit her lip. I knew she wouldn't react but I had something that would make her react. I pulled her panties down her thighs and grabbed the base of her butt plug. Her head shot up as she looked towards her husband.

What would he think? Why did she care? I rotated the plug and tugged at it causing her to begin to shudder on my lap. I then spanked her hard for several minutes leaving her ass a nice bright shade of red.

I then pushed her off my lap and once again tell her, "let him take your plug out". She knew better than to say or indicated anything as she moved to her husband. She was embarrassed as she turned saying. "Please take my plug out as my master has ordered". Her husband's eyes were wide as he reached for the base of the butt plug.

I sat watching the scene in front of me. You were standing in heels and nylons in front of your husband. He was sitting there looking at his wife like it was the first time. He slowly ran his hand up the back of her long leg. I could see the goose bumps running up and down it he smiled. One part of me wanted to jump up and slap his hand away and take her. I had to control that part through and let this happen.

His hand reached her ass cheek and squeezed she whipped her head around saying stop playing around and take the plug out of my ass. He spread her cheeks, leaned down to see the base of the plug. He gently touched it and she shuddered saying, "oh gawd sir, please don't have him do this. Her husband looked nervously to me and I said have you ever seen a butt plug not he answered.

Take her to your bathroom, have her stand in the tub, bend over and spread her legs. Then grab the plug. Slowly twist it back and forth a few times and then pull it free. You will have to pull firmly, to start to clear the bulb of the plug. Once clear it will pretty much come out on its own. Don't be surprised if she shits too. It's a natural thing after having one in for as long as she had it in her. Rinse her off and then bring her back here. Can you do that, I asked.

He looked from me to her and back to me ok. Standing he followed her out of the room. I listened to her heels clicking on the hard wood floor as they climbed some stares and then entered a bathroom. I couldn't hear anything over the music but I'm sure there was some talking going on. I could just imagine what it was. You never let me play with your ass. Do you like it? Well tonight might be his lucky night.

I could hear water running and chuckled. A few minutes later I could hear her screaming don't touch me you fucking prick. He didn't say you could fuck me. Stop goddamn it there was a lot of shuffling and scrapping until I heard her heels moving down the hall quickly. She came back into the room looking flushed and excited. She was wearing a robe and heels. Looking up at her I said take the robe off. She slowly slipped it from her shoulders leaving her once again standing in front of me topless, but now wearing some panties. I frowned asking,"

What's with the panties"? She looked down saying sorry sir I just had to get away from him before he got too carried away. Take them off. She reached down, slipping her finger beneath the waist of the little panties and began moving her hips to the music. She slowly began doing one of the most erotic strip teases that I had ever seen. Her big tits standing proud with her nipples pointing to the ceiling.

Gawd I loved those tits. She knew it too and reached up squeezing them asking, "would master like to nibble his nipples". I smiled opening my arms and she slowly moved to me. Straddling my lap and grinding her wet bare pussy on my hard cock as she squeezed her tits asking, "Which would you like first Sir". I looked to her big right nipple and she leaned forward as I took it into my warm mouth. She wanted to reach up and grab my head to hold it to her but she knew better and tried to stay still.

Just then her husband came back in to the room. He stopped and watched his wife feeding her big tits to his hungry mouth. He wanted to be sucking those big nipples but he knew he wouldn't be able to. It had been such a long time since he had. He sat down and watched as his wife continued grinding along my leg. I stopped sucking and looked to the other nipple as she turned and fed it to me. After a few minutes of sucking, I popped it free from my hungry mouth.

I reached around and squeezed her sweet ass. It brought a squeal from her as she tries to stand up. Getting to her shaky legs she stepped back and looked down. Quickly turning around, she smiled having noticed the big wet stain she had left on my trousers. I looked down and groaned "gawd you have one hot wife". Looking over to her husband he just shrugged saying "yeah I guess".

I could sense that he was feeling a lot of jealousy. "Why don't you head back to your room"? He looked from me to his sexy wife still dancing to the music. Gawd she could move. He then looked back at me saying "ok, night baby". She didn't even acknowledge him as she turned back to me. Grinding her pussy and once again dropping to a squat with her legs together. As she caught my eyes, she smiled a mischievous smile and opened them. Her pussy was open and wet. I swear it was close to dripping.

I'm so horny sir she whispered as she slid a finger through her lips and slowing into her pussy. She began fucking her finger with slow movements of her hips all the while looking me in the eye. Then she pulled her finger free. Standing, she slowly made her way to me and asked "Sir would you like a taste". "Did he cum in you"? Her eyes widened as she looked sown, "Sir I couldn't stop him". You want me to taste his cum and yours. Her excitement was building quickly and I knew that when I allowed her too, that she would cum as she never had before.

Opening my mouth I held out my tongue. I could hear her breathing coming in gasps as she brought her finger to my lips and slowly rubbed it over them. Sir can I get more. Yes. She quickly dipped her finger back into her hot pussy for a few minutes then brought it back to my lips and watched as she smeared her cum covered fingers across my lips. My tongue slipped out and around her finger gleaning it as she gasped "oh gawd sir".

Dance some more for me, I commanded. She turned then I swallowed the cum mixture. She began once again dancing.

Husbands view

I still can't believe that I agreed to the terms he had sent me, well there wasn't much I could do about them one way or the other. Somehow he had gotten complete control of my wife. She had to cut me off and was now his. When they drove up I peaked out the upstairs window and watched them. They seemed to talk a few minutes before getting out.

Then I ran downstairs and waited. I heard them come in and asked is that you honey. She answered it was and I told her to come into the den she walked in with him. She introduced us and he didn't acknowledge me. It make me feel so small. He wasn't a big man but he was big enough. He looked to be in his 40s or 50s maybe. Hair cut short but with a bit of gray to it. I could see why she had fallen for him. He was attractive but there was something else about him.

I watched him toughing her and he dismissed me. I wanted to take my wife and tell him to leave but I didn't. I walked to the guest room and waited. I listened to them talk and cold hear her groans and moans. She was turned on and I hadn't seen that in a long time. Then I heard him call me back in.

Walking into the room I see my wife dancing topless in front of him. What's going on in here I asked. Her big gorgeous tits out with her nipples so stiff. Gawd I hadn't been able to tough them in so long. I wanted to grab them, squeeze and chew on those stiff nipples. As I was watching her I heard him say she needs someone to dance with I moved towards her and she opened her arms. Wrapping my arms around her I pulled her tight or tried to. She kept pushing me away every time my shirt would brush her nipples. Gawd they were so had.

7

I reached down and tried to grab her tight ass but this caused her to groan louder and push me away harder.

She moved to the table and pulled out a chair. Pointing to it she tells me sit down and I'll give you a lap dance. I almost came in my pants as I moved to the chair and sat down. She slowly and seductively moved to me and started grinding her tight body against me. My dreams were coming true except for that asshole sitting on the couch stroking his dick as he watched. Still those big nipples kept drawing my attention and I so wanted to suck them.

As one got close enough I reached up and sucked it hard between my lips. She gasped, pulled and telling me gawd damn it. I'm not your play toy. I'm my masters and started dancing again. She moved to in front of him and squatted giving him a view I'm sure, of her very wet and excited pussy. I continued watching her tease him, and him stroking his dick running down his pants leg. Yea I guess he was bigger than me but damn she was my wife.

I heard him say let him take your plug out I watched as my wife turned to me with a concerned look on her face. She walked to me and turned away bending at the hip she reaches and grabs he knees. That's when I notice the plug in her ass. My hand is shaking as I reach up toughing the base of it. She squeals asking sir please don't let him do this I then run my hands up her long legs until I reach her ass. As I do, I hear him telling us what to do.

She stands up and starts walking towards the stairs, to her bathroom. I stand and follow her. Watching her incredible ass as it wobble this ways and that. Once upstairs she goes into the bathroom where she is standing in her tub. I slowly approach her as she bends over placing her hands on the wall pushing that ass out to me. I reach between her cheeks and twist the base as he suggested.

Then I pull on the base and push it back cussing he knees to buckle and her to say stop it you idiot and do as you wore told. I then grabbed the base and pulled until the huge bulb of the plug slipped from her tight ass. It slowly slipped further and further out until it dropped into the tub. I couldn't believe how fucking big it was. Then looking back I could still see her asshole opened up and a little dribble of shit coming out of it.

I reach over turn on the shower wand and rinse her clean. Once done she quickly steps out of the tub and moves into her room where I follow. She's my wife damn it and I am going to get some of that right now. As he was slipping her nylons off. I moved up behind her and pushed her over the chair she was standing before.

I quickly dropped my pants and shoved my cock balls deep into her. She cussed don't touch me you fucking prick he didn't say you could fuck me. Stop gawd damn it I had been so excited by the night activities that I didn't last but a few strokes before I was cumin in her hot pussy she gave me a nasty look.

She slipped on a pair of panties to keep the cum from running down her legs and headed back downstairs. I fell down into the chair catching my breath. Gawd she is a good fuck. I walked back into the room to find my wife straddling his lap letting him suck her big nipples and was loving it. Then she stood up she left a big wet spot on his trousers. I smiled knowing it was our cum. I wanted her. I wanted her badly. She was my fucking wife and she was letting him enjoy her.

I guess the way I was looking at my wife gave me away. I heard him saying gawd you have such a hot wife. I answered him without even knowing what I was saying yeah I guess. Then he said time for you to go to your room I was watching her moving and could feel my dick getting hard again. Gawd could she move. He cleared his throat and I said night baby, turned and walked down the hall to my room. Shutting the door I could still head the music and knew she was still dancing for him. Shit I wish I could have watched a bit more but maybe later her sill include me. He said he would.

Masters view

I sat back enjoying the incredible show she was giving me. She was moving like I had seldom seen... smiling I say go up and change into something more appropriate. Her eyes widened as if I had reached out and squeezed her tits yes master. She turned and started out of the room I could once again hear the click clack of her heels on the floor and stairs and then the roof above me. Evidently her room was above the den.

I could hear her moving around the room. She was still dancing to the music as she dressed. I got up, went to the kitchen and fixed a couple of drinks. Reaching into my pocket I took out the vile opening it took one pill out and dropped it into her drink closing the vile I slipped it back in to my slacks. Swirling the glass I watched it dissolve and smiled thinking, a little added incentive wouldn't hurt. I could see her squirting her cum again and again like she had in the car. Good thing it was a rental because someone was going to smell her sex when I returned it. Shen came hard and soaked the seat. Walking back into the den I could her above dancing around. I placed her drink on the table and mine on the end table. Turning, I walked back down the hall and knocked on the door to the guest room. He opened it with anticipation. I laughed saying relax I will come get you when it's time.

Here take one of these to make sure our will be ready. I handed him the 100mg Viagra. He took it and looked at it. Take it now. He popped it into his mouth and swallowed. Good don't beat your meat. I want it all for her. Understand. He nodded his head. Smiling you can leave your door cracked so you can watch a little.

I then turned away and walked back into the den. I took my drink and sipped it. The dancing upstairs shad stopped and now I could hear the click clank of heels coming back down the hall. Down the stairs down the hall. I turned away and looked out a window as she entered the room. I heard her stop as she walked in.

Slowly I turn around to see the perfect submissive before me. She was down on her knees, head down legs spread with her hands at her side. I smiled and said show me. She wanted to smile so big but held it back. She knew I would love her outfit. She had saved it for the one chance she might get to wear it.

Standing I took in every delicious inch of her. On her feet were thigh high black leather 6" stiletto heeled boots. I could feel my cock throb continuing on up I noticed she was wearing red fishnet stocking s that lead up to a black leather corset with red trim. The cups of the corset wore open with her heavy tits being held up and available. I thought I was going to cum in my fucking pants. She was a dream come true.

Continuing up I see she is wearing the black leather chocker collar that I had given her. Hanging from it was the medallion that read her masters. Her lips were painted a bright red. She was also wearing a black leather red trimmed blind fold. Smiling I moved a step closer to her.

I knew all her senses were heightened now and could see her draw a big breath. Her tits heaved with the breath. She could smell my cologne and knew I had come closer. She didn't know exactly how close but the scent aroused her. Her hands still hung from her side and I could see them trembling. She was waiting for m approval or disapproval.

Turn around slowly I instructed. She took a deep breath which almost took mine as I watched those gorgeous tits raise and fall I swear her nipples could cut glass. Slowly se began turning around and once glancing away from me she stopped. Bend over I instructed. I could see her thigh trembling as she slowly and very seductively leaned forward from the waist she continued until her hands touched the floor. Gawd she was limber.

Her legs were spread and I had to grab my cock. The corset was crotch less and her wet open pussy was revealed for me. Gawd I wanted to rip my pants off and shove my cock deep in that hot hole. Her ass had recovered and closed back up but I knew it would be ready for the fucking that was ahead.

Turn around and face me I instructed I then stepped very close to her I could smell her perfume now and it was intoxicating. She slowly eased up and slowly tuned around. Her tits heaving with each breath as she now knew I was lose. She could feel my presence through her body and she could smell my scent...

Did he approve? Gawd I hope he very excited because I am literally dripping, she thought. She shuddered as she could almost feel my tough before I touched her. Reaching up I gently cupped her heaving tits weighing those gorgeous boobs, letting my thumbs flick across her very sensitive nipples. She had her head down in the submissive attitude and it was taking all her strength no to cry out, oh gawd pinch them.

I could almost read her mind and took each nipple between my fingers. As she felt my fingers wrapping around each nipple she wanted to scream. Trembling waiting for me to pinch and pull at them she was going insane. I let my fingers take possession of each nipple and just put the slightest of pressure on them. Her whole body was trembling, just squeeze for gawd sake, squeeze hard she wanted to cry.

Smiling I released her nipples and stepped away from her. oh gawd whit is he doing to me she was pleading. Her whole body slumped and I instructed, stand tall, shoulders back.

She knew what I wanted and did as instructed. She was proud that she could dive me to such extremes. She had never had such a power over someone who she had given all power to. Standing thee now she knew her big tits were thrust forward and out. She knew her pussy would almost be in view with her legs spread. Standing completely still she waited/ his sent wasn't as strong so now he was standing away from her somewhere. Where?

Her sense of hearing caught the sound. He was opening his slacks. She could hear his zipper slowly opening. She didn't want to breathe for fear she wouldn't hear everything. Then she heard his slacks rustling down his thighs and his belt hit the floor. His cloths being kicked off. Next was the soft rustle of his shirt being taken off and was thrown on the floor. She had lost control of her breathing now and was coming in short deep gasps. Her gorgeous tits shaking with each breath.

8

Stepping over to my drink I sipped it watching this incredible woman before me. Gawd I wish I had a video of this. Turning I noticed her husband peaking from around the door. He looked with disbelief of what his wife was doing. Fuck she looked good. She looked better than good. She looked like a fucking goddess. His goddess. He then noticed me watching him and ducked back down the hall and waited.

Reach your hand out I instructed. She slowly brought her hand up I walked over, took her drink and handed it to her. Drink I said. Then went over to the chair she had placed for her husband, and sat down. My cock was hanging down between my legs as I said, remove the blindfold and dance for me.

She took a large gulp of her drink and then whipped the blindfold off. Her excitement running wild in her as she wanted to see his approval. She took another gulp of her drink and then turned to place her empty glass on the table. She then began moving to the music. Letting her excitement and the music flow through her body. She was going to make this night so special for him no matter what it took.

He smiled to himself, glancing up at the clock. It would be about 30-45 minutes before the ecstasy to take effect. Looking back at his gorgeous lady he watched her moving. His cock getting harder and harder as she moved.

Every time she turned she would glance to see if he was enjoying it and when she saw him responding she knew. Stopping facing him she once again squatted down with her legs together. Then shyly looking up into his eyes she asked sir. She could see in his eyes that he wanted her like he had never wanted her before. Show me I instructed. She reached down taking each knee in her hands and slowly opened her legs. She kept her eyes on his as she showed him how excited she was. Her breath was deeper and deeper as she waited.

Don't move I commanded. Her eyes widened as she didn't know what to expect now. She watched me stand up and slowly move towards her. Oh gawd no he can't I won't be able to stop.

Sliding slowly on my back I moved until she squatted wet pussy was just above me. Don't you fucking move and don't look down. Do you hear me? Yes Sir. She kept her hands on her knees, spread wide as she looked straight ahead. She could feel my breath on her wet swollen lips. If he does I'm going to cum. I can't cum. He hasn't said I could cum. Oh gawd this is driving me crazy.

I slowly stick my tongue out and very tenderly run it along a swollen lip. I can hear her whimpering but I continue on. My tongue continued along her lip until I reached her hard clit. It was swollen beyond belief as my tongue softly caressed it. I softly kissed it and then slipped from beneath her. Standing up I moved back and took my drink.

While I was facing away from her she looked down and gave a soft gasp as she noticed a small pool of liquid on the floor between her legs. Oh gawd please sir let me cum, she wanted to scream. Stand up and continue dancing for me I instruct as I move back to the chair and sit down. Come dance for me I instruct her.

With my drink in one hand and waving her note in the other, I made my way down the hall to the open door. I paused at the door imagining what might await me beyond that door. Her note said I had prepared a room for your enjoyment. Now that was interesting. This would give me a glimpse into just what she thought I enjoyed. I anticipated it to be, for her enjoyment though and not particularly mine. Oh I enjoyed taking her to her limits and then past only to bring her back gain. That was for her enjoyment though.

I tried smile came to my face as I wondered if there was a beach beyond that door. With warm waves lapping at the shore. With an even warmer sun high in the sky. No I knew there wasn't but it was ok. This was who I am to her. We had our separate lives and didn't interfere in wither. I had gotten into the lifestyle with excited vigor. I had learned from masters hot to find what made a submissive want to please. I had used it to my advantage many times. Now through the years were growing on me and I wasn't a young man anymore.

I stood at the door and looked down the stairs. There was a man down there that seemed to want nothing more than to be with his wife. Of course I recognized that it was just him being horny but still that was a start. Maybe tonight I could show him what his wife was wanting, when she has been craving. No I couldn't. He just wanted a piece of ass and that's not what this type of relationship is about in the long run.

Looking back into the room, I could see a bright light focused on something behind the door. If I could let someone, that would be her. Somehow restrained and waiting, oh the waiting was special. When she knows I there but doesn't know where. She begins breathing faster. Her senses reach out for any sign. It's amazing to watch. The bright light would work almost like a blindfold to her. She wouldn't be able to see anyone standing behind it. She would know they were there but she still couldn't be sure.

I stepped onto the room and looked to right to see her standing there. I could feel my cock getting thick again it was becoming harder and harder for me to keep the distance between us. I wanted to touch her. To run my hands along her neck, across her jaw, across the lips, down her neck, across her tits, down her stomach and over her mound. I wanted to hear her moan and I wanted to feel her wanting me. That wasn't good for me. Shaking my head I looked at her. She was wearing some kind of red full body fishnet suit with some slutty heels, a pair of black string panties and her choker collar.

Her nipples were still very hard and clearly poking through the net. She kept turning her head trying to see if I was there. Nice I said sir are you pleased? Yes my pet I'm pleased. Glancing around I see the cables attached to her wrists through the ceiling hooks and back down behind. Looking down at her ankles I see the m connected to the walls on each side of her. Noticing the other eye hooks I see that you could suspend someone on the back or ace down very easily. Who did this? A friend of mine and I did it sir.

Looking around the room I see what someone might think is a padded bench but it's used for body support when the sub is lowered into a horizontal position. Walking slowly around the room, I notice a huge wardrobe. Opening the door, I see a very nice selection of whips, floggers, crops, various forms of clips, dildos and vibrators. Also I notice several hoods and blindfolds as well as ball gags... those might come handy s the night progresses I chuckle. How much have you used. Sir don't make me tell you, please sir.

I smile, I've known for some time that she had been seeing and experiencing other Dom's. It was against all our agreements but she was like a child wanting to know and experience more and more. She needed someone younger to serve her better. I knew it and had been slowly pulling my attention away from her.

This meeting was the first in several months. Tonight I was going to cut the choker from her neck and release her. Before I did though, I was going to have one more night of fucking. She had always been interested in double penetration but was Leary to involve anyone else. So I used toys with her. She always got off hard but tonight I was going to bring her husband in and we were going to DP her. I suspect the she had already experienced it but tonight I was going to experience it with her. Plus with the added stimulation of the drugs. She would enjoy it beyond anything she normally would have.

Moving to one wall, I slip about a foot and slack in the ankle cable. So tell me moving to the other wall I slip a foot of slack into that ankle cable. She drops her head, sir my friend wanted to help me prepare this for you. We needed some technical advice and she got him to come over. They tied me and spent the day enjoying me. I had moved behind her and grabbed the cable connected to her wrists. Pulling sharply, I lift her from the floor just till her tiptoes touch. She tried to kick but it just caused her shoes to slip from her feet and clatter to the floor

So when I put the collar on you what did it mean? She could feel my breath on her neck as I spoke and her body was trembling please sir I'm sorry. Standing behind her, I reach out and run my hands down her arms, her tits and down her hips. HMMMM such a sweet thing, I whisper; with a louder voice I say what did it mean? It means that I am your and no one is to approach me without your consent. But I wasn't wearing my collar sir. How did I know she would say that? Sometimes it was like dealing with a small child.

I walked back to the wardrobe and selected a flogger, a ball gag and a blindfold. He didn't ask if you were collared. Sir please. Walking up behind, I slipped the blind fold over her eyes. As I did I could feel the tears on her cheeks, she knew she had done very wrong and there was no taking it back. Our bond was a trust. A trust she put in me to never hurt her or make her feel inadequate. A trust I put in her that she would never allow herself to be used by anyone other than me. Sir. Shhhh as I popped the ball gag across her lips. Sir please wait let me explain.

I reached around grabbing her jaw and firmly placing the ball gag in her mouth s she struggled to talk. Now all I could hear was gurgle. Picking up the flogger, I strike the wall several times hard. Her body goes taunt with anticipation. You broke my trust... and I swatted her sweet ass with the flogger. Not as hard as I had hit the wall but hard enough to keep her attention. Moving around to her other side I swat her ass again and again and gain. If one leaving her screaming out into the room. Her legs now kicking trying to stay on her tiptoes. Each swat sent her swinging though she was muttering.

Walking back around the wardrobe, I looked around and found several rolls of tape some scissors. Picking the scissors up, I walked back around behind her. Leaning forward I ask do you know what today is. She nods her head yes. 3 years ago today I put this collar on you. Slipping my fingers between your neck and it/ I pull it slipping the scissors around it saying and tonight I release you as I snip the leather collar in to. She begins mumbling very fast and shaking her head no, no, no, as the collar slips from her neck and falls down across her tits and hit the floor.

Her head drops in total submission now as he knows there is nothing she can do. What's been done is done. I move back around and place the scissors. Moving to a wall I untie an ankle cable and move back several spots and the retie it. Moving over to the other wall I do the same. This has her pitched forward a little more than 45 degrees. Still not too much pressure on her wrists and shoulders.

Going back to the wardrobe I select a nice leather crop and move in front of her. I've given you two hits of ecstasy tonight. They aren't real high doses but enough to make you want to fuck anything that you can get your hungry pussy on. Taking the crop I flick it across on of her extended nipples causing her to shriek loudly. Then I do the other nipple. You will know what's going on but you won't be able to stop yourself.

She lost her stuff and seems that each time has to be taken just a little further, but tonight the ecstasy will do that without having to be put to those extremes. Moving behind him I begin flicking the crop up her thigh until I reach her dripping pussy and then flick it across her clit causing her to jerk and moan as she squirts across the floor beneath her. Her body shuddering as she achieves a massive orgasm. As she seems to be relaxing I begin again moving up the other thigh and ending once again with several flicks across her clit.

She is screaming into the gag as her body gives in. I move back around and place the crop back in the wardrobe. I then reach over and cut the lights down dim. I don't need them so bright now with her blindfolded, I walk up to her and brush the seat soaked hair from her face. I smile saying you one had a fantasy that you were chicken to try. Do you remember? It was a DP. Well tonight it will be realized. She tensed up and began shaking her head as she realized what it meant. If that damn gag wasn't in her mouth she would tell that she had already experienced it. That she didn't want me to let him spoil this night for us. She couldn't though and her body came alive with desire.

Gawd she wanted me to tough her she wanted me to flick that crop across her nipples again. Fuck the drugs won't let me think straight. What have I done? I found the stereo and cut it on. Not only to give me has something to enjoy but to help drown out her screamed. I slid the bench around under her. I then slowly lowered her wrist cables don until she was resin got the padded bench. Looking around I see the keys to the locks on the table and move around to them. I them move back to her.

Unlocking on wrist and then locking it to the lower ring on the bench I then do the same for the other wrist. Once they are secured I do her ankles and same the same. Leaving her now tied to the bench face down. The dench is actually sculptured in that is wide at the base and narrows up to the head. Giving maximum support for her hips and leaving her tits hanging for maximum pleasure. Her head is also free to move with a small pad lower down if she were to pass out.

Whoever she used for these did very well. She is positioned perfectly for whatever fun I wanted to do. I could take her ass or her pussy. Her tits hanging would fill with blood causing her nipples to become super sensitive. Oh and her mouth was the perfect level to slide a nice hard cock in. I'm standing behind her, open my jeans, pull my hard cock out and rub it across her wet slit causing her to jerk and hump against the bench. Grabbing her hips I shove in with one delicious shove until I'm balls deep in her quivering cunt.

I reach up and unhook her ball gag and she spits it out screaming oh fuck, fuck me goddamn you fuck me.

I reach down and around to cup both hanging tits, taking her extended nipples between my fingers rolling them, no don't, please, oh gawd, fuck me she continues yelling. I slowly withdraw my wet cock from her pussy but continue rolling her nipples. No, sir, shit I'm going to cum, fuck me, please fuck me. Leaning over her I whisper to her call your husband no gawd just fuck me. No until you call your husband and with that I give one hard squeeze to her nipples and pull away.

This leaves her humping against the bench. Trying to get some pressure on her clit but she can't but still she tries. I stand stroking my wet cock watching her trying to fuck the bench. Tell him to come fuck you. No you bastard I won't do it, please fuck me you know you want to. How do you know he isn't already here? She freezes her movements no he can't be, no just fuck me you mother fucker. She begins humping against the bench again saying, you know you want it, I've watched you all night and you want me bad.

Take me if you are man enough but I won't call that asshole to come fuck me.

Smiling I say we will see about that, I walk back to the wardrobe and pick of a container of clothes pins and a small stool. I walk back and set the stool down loudly so she knows what I'm doing. Her head turns hearing he noise and processing what it could have been. Then I drop the container of clothes pins next to it and move quietly around her. She has that too and stops moving. What are you doing? I say I am not doing anything her head jerks around to where my voice came from and now she doesn't know for sure he isn't here.

You're just playing games with me. You know you want to fuck this sweet pussy. Come on, I want to feel that talented tongue of yours again fucking me. You know you want to taste it. Its sweet baby I promise. I'm ready to squirt all over you again. Come on baby, mommas got what you want. Proceed I say and then swat that perfect ass with a paddle I had picked up. Shit, you mother fucker I then move back around sitting on the stool and reach for a hanging tit. Grabbing it, I reach for a clothes pin and place it about 3 inches from her nipple. I then place 3 more in a circle around the tit. I then do the other just the same and quickly move away.

Stop for gawd sake you asshole as she begin humping against the bench again. She is slowly losing control now as he mind tries to regain its command. Moving back around I pick the paddle up and smack each cheek 4 times, just like the pins on her tits. We're waiting. No I won't I know you want this pussy for yourself. Take it. Fuck me.

Try and make me cum if you can,

While she was spitting out her rage, I moved back to my stool and grabbed a tit. OH no she screamed as I placed 3 pins around the edge of each nipple. Her body is withering on the bench now trying to shake the pins loose but not able to. My tits, oh gawd my tits she wailed. I moved back around and placed 3 smacks across her each cheek this time. Mother fucker, when I get loose I'm going to go downstairs and fuck my husband.

I'm going to give him all this hot pussy and my tight ass and leave you up here to jerk off thinking about all this pussy you could he had. Now fuck me she screamed. She was madly humping against the bench now.

I turned and went back to the wardrobe fixing my next treat for her. As I did I noticed her husband at the door watching with wide eyes and stroking his had cock. I smiled and signaled for him to keep quiet.

What are you doing now? I swear if you do anything else I'm going to fuck him till he can't walk and leave you to play with your own dick. She threatened. I look at him and his eyes were as big as half dollars. Evidently he hadn't ever heard her in this state. I loved it when she got to this point and I could see he did too. I tied the 5lb weights to the cables and attached them to the clips. I then screwed the clips down as tight as they would go.

I signaled him over and told him to go stand behind her and when I nod my head you smack that as with that paddle one hard time on each cheek... got it. He nodded his head. Remember no matter what she says. Do as I tell you I say. Taking a clip I attach it to my jeans and drop the weight. It doesn't pull fee.

My gawd my tits baby. If you don't take those pins off I'm not going to let you fuck me. You know you want to. That dick nice and had and wanting some of her sweet pussy. Take them off baby. Fucker take them off, she screams. I'm not playing asshole. STAR, STAR, STAR she hollers. I pause this the first time she has our used the safe word. Trouble was she had violated the rules of the collar so I wasn't no longer compiled to comply with her safe word.

Sitting down on the stool I leaned forward and took her head in my hands. Moving close to her ear I whisper, since you violated our trust agreement I can't trust you, you can't trust me and released her. Her head dropped oh gawd, my tits, I' call him just take the pins off. I knew she was playing a game but it did surprise me that she would go all the way to using her safe word. Oh well in for a penny in for a dollar.

I reach out and position the clips beneath each hanging nipple they have begun to turn purple but I know I still have a few minutes before I would have to release her. I time her breaths and on an intake I open both clips quickly and attach them to her nipples. This brings a long slur of obscenities from her, son of a bitch, oh gawd you ae going to pull them off, and she began calling or her husband. Begging for him to come fuck her I nodded... as the paddle cashed down on her as cheek the 5lb weights pulled heavily on her already tested tits.

You mother fuckers, I'm not going to fuck either one of you now as her body begins shaking uncontrollably. I look up and see she is squirting long streams of cum across the floor. Shit. Would one of you queers just stick your dick in and fuck me, she pleaded. He looked at me and I nodded he quickly moved up behind her even before she had stopped squirting and slammed his cock deep into her quivering pussy.

OHHHHHHHHHHH fuck yeah. Fuck me you bastard. Come on you can do better than that, she goaded. He was slamming his cock in and out as hard as he could. Gripping her hips and snarling as he fucked his wife. You've got to be my husband, cause you can't fuck worth a shit. Come on you pussy, fuck me she continued. Raising he head in my direction she says, you know what you've got this to do shut me up you sorry bitch.

I reached down and pulled the blindfold from her eyes. She shook her head and then looked up at me. The lust and excitement in her eyes told me what I needed to know. Well if you are going to stuff that little dick of yours down my throat, at least get one of the dildos from the cabinet and let me suck it she dared. She then watched as I unbuckled my jeans and slid them down my thighs, stepping out of them. Smiling she turned her head back towards her husband saying goddamn it you fuck like a little boy, fuck me lie a man.

I then grabbed two hands full of hair and held her head as I brought my cock to her lips. She kept them closed mumbling no I want a big dick to suck, no. I reached down and pinched her nose causing her to open her mouth with a gasp and I slid my cock in. she.

She then went to work. Gawd this girl could suck a dick. I released her head enjoying but she spit me out saying, you want this mouth bitch you got to earn it. Gawd I loved it when she got this excited......

Stepping back could see her husband fucking away between her thighs. I could hear the slap, slap, slap.as he fucked his wife for all he was worth. The room smelled of sex now. Her body was glistening with sweat but she wasn't about to give in not yet.

Turning her head back to her husband, she demanded, come on little boy can't you make me cum. Bet I can make you cum before you make me. I watched her face and saw her concentrating and knew what she was doing. She was squeezing his cock as it slammed in to her. His head shot up, goddamn what is she doing as he tried to get back control. It was too late though.

She looked up into my eyes with a smile on her face saying don't you wish this was your dick. He is going to cum. I can feel his dick swelling.

Watch. I looked back to see him slumping over her as his body jerked and finally he hell back. Stumbling saying she never fucked me like that. I looked down into her eyes as she said hmmmm you want creamy seconds.

I sat down in front of her and reached under to begin removing the clothes pins from her hanging tits. Once I had them all removed and just the weighted clips on her grossly extended nipples she groaned be gentle with momma's tits you bastard. I don't know if I will ever let you play with them again. I smiled and then slapped each hanging tit bringing holy fuck you freak, stop, gawd please stop. I reached beneath her and she dropped her head watching as I released each clip and her tits snapped back shit you dastard.

I then moved down and under her until I was looking up at a hanging tit. Oh gawd, no don't you fucking dare so it. I clamped my lips around a swollen purple nipple and sucked hard.

I could feel her body trying to pull away but there was nowhere for her to go. NOOOOOOOOOO STTTTOOOOOOPPPPPP!!! I released her nipple with a loud smack and moved around to the other side her eyes followed my every move and as I reached up to suck the other nipple she cried, suck momma's tits you bitch. I'm not going to let you cum all night for this. I sucked her tender sensitive nipple for about 2 or3 minutes before releasing it with a loud pop.

I stood up and moved back behind her. She was twisting her head back and forth trying to see what I was going to do. Oh so now you think you can get some of this hot pussy. If I wasn't tied down you wouldn't get it. I reached down and picked up the paddle her husband had used. I then laid it across her ass. Her head shot around oh gawd no, now enough is enough. Don't you fucking dare! No sooner than the word dare got out of her lips than I delivered a vicious attack on her up turned ass.

I landed 3 quick blows that left her jerking hard at her binds. For saying such nasty threats, and I delivered 3 more smacks on her ass. It was glowing redder tan her little body suit now. Not got anything left to say you fucking nasty slut. I delivered three more smacks causing her to scream out. Please oh gawd Sir. I'm sorry, I'll do anything please no more. I delivered 5 hard smacks to her ass causing her to actually slide forward on the floor. Mother Mary of gawd please no more sir, STAR, STAR, STAR...

Smiling I turned to her husband saying star was our safe word. Once she used it, it was supposed to stop whatever was going on and allow her to regain her composure. I then turned the paddle around and held the handle out to her husband. But you don't have a safe word, do you. He smiled and she whipped her head around No, No, NOOOO please NO not him. He then unleashed a blistering of her ass. Leaving her panting wildly draped over the bench. Oh gawd Sir please no more I've got to rest

THE RELEASE

I looked at her husband and nodded. I took and walked over to the wardrobe and laid it down. Then I looked back to her husband saying you can release her now. I'm going down to fix myself another drink, would you like one. He nodded saying I'd like a beer from the fridge. I turned facing her and tucked my thick cock back into my jeans, zipped them up and buttoned them. Her breathing was of someone who had just ran al long race. Deep and ragged but her eyes were alive. Sir may I have a drink.

That woman amazed me at times. She could be driven to such extremes and still regain her self the next second. It always drove me so crazy when I was with her. She could be such a slut, then back to the sub and then back still to the tough woman she projected to the public. I didn't know which I liked best but the slut had to be close. I smiled and walked out of the room. Downstairs the music was still playing and I made the drinks and got his beer. As I reached the foot of the stairs I could hear the slap slap, slap, slap, coming from the room.

Oh gawd you ass hole, he said and release me not fuck me. I grinned and sat down on the steps and sipped my drink and I listened to him fuck his wife. Slap. Slap slap, as his hips drove his cock deep into her. Cum for me you dick. Fill that pussy with cum cause this is going to be the last time you get any of it. I heard him groaning and figured he was doing just that. Now let me up you shit, before he comes back.

Smiling I realized the two hits had brought her to the edge of being the slut and the sub. Seemed the slightest stimulation would bring the slut to the surface but once completed, the sub world re-appear. I could hear he locks being loosened and her groan as she slowly to her feet. You two did a number on me that time. I will get you back though you fucker. Tell him I've gone to take a shower and I will meet him outside at the hot tub I started up the stairs and when I reached the top she came out of the room heading towards hers.

Her eyes shot down to the ground and she stood still. Sir I'm going to take a shower and get cleaned up, please meet me at the hot tub. I reached out to hand her the drink but she moved into my arms. Pressing her necked body to mine as she whispered I want to fuck you so bad. I leaned back and she took her drink. As she did I reached out to hold her tit. She stoop perfectly still as I ran my finger across where the pins had been attached then gently across her nipple as she closed her eyes saying I'm fine sir. I grin and give the nipple a soft squeeze causing her to whisper.

I know you still want a piece of this. She then pulled away from me quickly and headed to her room. I watched that fine ass wiggle as she walked away and groaned, shit, you've got one hell of a wife. Her husband was standing in the doorway and I handed him his beer.

As she reached her door, she turned saying I'm not his I'm yours. My face turned serious as I reached behind me taking out the cut collar and showing it to her again. No you aren't mine. Her face dropped as she reached up to her neck. She had for gotten about that but now she remembered. I could see in her eyes there was a huge battle going on. Suddenly though she looked up into my eyes saying I'm going to take a quick shower. Show him where the hot tub is. And turned walking away.

He looked at me saying come on we can go out this way so are we still going to DP her, he asked. He was a man who had just fucked his wife two times and had abused her sweet ass and now was asking if he was going to get to fuck her again. She's your wife. What do you want to do? I ask as we walk out onto the deck. It's a beautiful night. The sky is full of stars and it's very mild. Perfect weather we walk around the deck until I see the covered hot tub.

He then goes about uncovering it and starting it up.

Inside, she slipped into the bathroom. But picked her phone up on the way in. quickly dialing he fiend she waited. Hey what are you doing nothing how about you. Having a party and I want you to come over right now. Right now. Right now and be quick. Come up to my room. Ok I'm on my way. She then slips into the shower and rinses off the sweat from her body. She inspects her tits and can't help but groan as the stimulation gets to her. Fuck I am going to teach that bastard a lesson tonight. He has fucked me twice already and I'm going to fuck him now. She then rinses off and steps out of the shower. She then digs through her drawer of bikinis for the two she was looking for.

Finding them she stands up and begins slipping it on hen the door opens and her friend steps in.

Shit Beth you scared the crap out of me. Bah laughed saying ok so what s up baby girl she then tossed Beth the other bikini saying. Get dressed we are going to have some fun.

She took the suit and looking at it sighed. I don't know about this. Ah come on. Look at me I'm wearing this one. Stepping back Beth groaned. Hummm. Do I get to play too? Smiling she says sure baby. We can play too. With that Beth begins to strip and slip into the tiny piece of material that might cover nipple and the bottoms are basically dental floss.

Beth ask what have you been drinking. Smiling she says just a couple drinks but a couple hits of ecstasy. Beth steps forward and runs her hands along her body until she is cupping her tits. Oh fuck Beth. Squeeze them... Beth smiles and squeezes her friend's tits and leans forward to share a soft passionate kiss. Can you get me a couple hits of the ecstasy too? Beth asked. Smiling she says let me go find out. I'll be right back.

She then moves out of the bathroom, grabs a robe hanging in her closet and steps through the French doors leading to the deck. Turning she sees us siting talking. Excuse me Sir, but could I talk to you for a minute. I look over at her husband and then back to her, privately please sir. I stand up and walk towards her. She turns and walks back to the doors to her room. At the sight of her husband, she stops and turns.

Slowly opening her robe to show me what she is wearing. I walk up to her smiling as she reaches out pulling me closer.

HMMMMM, is my baby still hungry for some pussy. I lean forward and softly kiss her neck as she reaches down gabbing my thickening cock, oh hell yea, momma wants this baby. I bite her neck and she pushes me away. Oh you are wanting to be naughty Sir I've asked a friend over and she is in the bathroom right now putting on her bikini. Sir can she have a couple hit of ecstasy please. I look towards the bathroom door and then back to her saying why no it's over in my slacks pocket, help yourself.

Thank you sir. We will make it worth your while, and moves back against me. Making sure she grinded her mound against my cock. I reached around squeezing her ass causing her to twist. I look worried at her and say in that case. I will need to watch her take the hits. She looks at me and then realizes, oh no sir I wouldn't slip them to you. No, I will need to see her take them or none. She sighs ok. Hang on.

I walk into the room and reach into my slacks pocket taking out the small vial. Opening it, I drop out 2 hits and then urn waiting for their return. The bathroom door opens and she steps out followed by

Beth. They both were wearing silky short robes pulled tight to their bodies. This is my friend Beth. Beth this is my. She stopped and looked to me and I grin, I'm glad to meet you Beth. Are you sure you want to take these. She glanced towards her and then back to me saying can I trust you. I smile saying sure you can. As I look at her big tits pushing through the thin robe. Ok then, she takes the two hits. I'll need to see you swallow them Beth. Oh ok can I have some of your drink. I handed her my drink and she takes both hits. How long before they take effect.

HMMMMM, about 45 minutes or so I would guess. I've never done them before but if it will make me feel as good as she is, then I'm good.

She had been watching us talk and could see me checking her fiend out. There was a part of her hat was very jealous of that and she couldn't control it.

Moving up to me she opens her robe and presses her nearly naked body against me asking. Can I have another please? I don't know you've already had two. Yea but hers will be taking effect about the time mine will be wearing off, she pouted. I opened the vial and take out the last hit saying your choice.

Snatching it quickly from my hand she popped it into her mouth. Grabbed my drink and chased it. Running her hand down my bare stomach and popping the button of my jeans loose. She whispers I still have had what you have for me yet.

Then she quickly stepped away leaving me almost breathless as she turned to Beth saying come on, we'll meet you out by the hot tub, and they walked out of the room. I turned and made my way back to my chair on the deck. He husband ask. What was that about? I tell him that she had invited Beth over and they were downstairs fixing dinks. He sat up in his chair. Beth with bit tits. I looked over at him saying, yea they looked pretty big. Holy fuck, he groaned as he rubbed his towel covered cock.

Down boy I thought you wanted to fuck your wife. Hell no, if Beth is here, I will take her and you can have the bitch. I sat back looking out into the night sky. How funny that was. Seems we are ready to give up what we have for something that we think is better. I couldn't count how many times husbands said they didn't care only to find them later wishing they hadn't given their wives up. Well this one would learn soon enough with her saying, I'm going to get even with him tonight. Meant what he suspected it meant,

We hear the click clank of heels on the deck and turn in that direction as they come around the corner. Even in the dim light they looked hot in the thin short robes and heels. She is carrying a pitcher and a beer. Beth is caring 3 glasses and a bucket of ice. Walking over to the table, they set the things down and she turns to husband saying, make yourself use full and cut on some music out here he is watching Beth's every move, hoping that those big tits would bop out of that robe. Hey dickless. He shakes his head saying what. How about some music. He stands up saying hi Beth... she runs saying hey. And tried to ignore him. He walked around the deck and left us alone.

She quickly moves around and sits on my lap and turns to me. Beth is going to help me get even with that asshole, please don't interfere. I look from he to Beth and back at he. How can I help he eyes widen and a big smile comes to those sweet lips as she reaches down and unties her robe. Reaching out she takes my hand and guides it inside the robe until I'm holding one of those bit tits of hers. I can feel the stiff nipple pressing against the tiny material trying to cover it. I squeeze her big tit as she says, just be your normal horny dominate self and I'll take good care of you. With that she leans down and we begin a long hot kiss.

Suddenly the quiet of the night is broken my music as she jumps saying that numb nut will wake every neighbor. She jumped up and rounded the corner leaving Beth and me alone. Shyly she looked at me I motioned for her to come sit in my lat. She looked the direction they had gone and then slowly moved around the table and onto my lap.

Untie your robe I instructed her. Her hands were starting to tremble as she untied the little belt. I then raise my hand saying well. She looked back down the deck and then reached out for my hand. Slowly she brought it inside her robe and onto her huge tit. She felt my cock flex and he eyes widened. I gently squeezed her tit and rolled he fat nipple between my fingers. She leaned her head forward with a groan, holy fuck.

How much time has it been? I would guess about 20 minutes but sense you took a double dose it might hit you faster. Have you eaten anything in a while? Oh no. are you getting excited I asked as I pinched her sighs no please don't but stops as my hand begins sliding down her body. Her eyes widen as I tell her open your legs. She reluctantly does as she is told and my finger s slip across her mound.

This time I groan, holy fuck you are soaked. As my fingers slide across and through her lips. Oh gawd, she wants him to fuck me but I don't want him too. As she pushed back against my fingers. I slide them up and find a fucking huge clit. It's got to be about the size of my thumb. Her head falls against mine as she breathes into my ear. I want to fuck her and I want you to fuck me. I smile and carefully begin stroking her hard clit like a little cock. Her hand shoots down grabbing minge making me stop saying not yet, please not yet.

I release her clit and slip her bottom back over it and pull my hand out of her robe joust about the time they come back around the corner. He is such a fucking klutz, and she stopped looking at her friend curled up in my lap. Her head laid over on my shoulder and obviously she had been enjoying herself. Will I see you two have got to know one another. Its then that I realized that she was jealous. Oh I was going to have fun with this. She pushed her shoulders back and opened he robe, dropping it down her shoulders. Now standing in front of me with that sexy ass string on and looking so fucking hot.

Beth looked up but his excitement had gotten the better of her. I nuzzled close to her ear saying. Doesn't she look good enough to eat? I could feel Beth shudder and knew she wanted her badly. Raising her forward I reached up and pulled her robe from her body leaving her sitting there with her nipples standing hard against the tiny bikini. She couldn't stand it. She quickly moved to the table saying let's get a couple of drinks and get in the tub. Beth slowly moved to her feet. A little unsteady in her high heels as she moved to the table and brushed up against her friend.

You aren't mad are you Beth asked. It's those hits they've got me so horny. Beth continued. She smiled as she poured the drinks and looked at her friend.no baby they are working on me to. She then reached over and pulled Beth to her to share a long kiss. When they separated, her husband was standing there with his tongue hanging out. She turned to him laughing. Stop you horny old fool. And held out a drink for me. I stood up and accepted the drink and watched as the two girls climbed into the tub.

Looking down at my jeans I asked, you have suits on, all I have are my jeans. She moved to the edge of the tub and reached out, here baby, let me help you off with them, we don't want to get them all wet. I moved closer to the tub and she reached out grabbing my jeans and pushing the zipper down. Then reaching around my waist and the pushing them off my hips. In doing so this caused her to have to lean out of the tub, leaving her big wet tits hanging for our enjoyment.

Once my jeans cleared my hips my hard cock sprang out. She quickly grabbed it stroking it slowly saying, I told you I wasn't going to let you cum tonight since you were so mean to me earlier, and she pushed away sitting back in the tub. I groaned and stepped up and into the tub. Beth was quick to move around to me saying, don't worry baby, and if she won't I certainly will, and grabbed my cock before I could sit down.

Her husband wanting in on the action stepped up to the tub saying, we'll all I have got is this towel. She wanted to play him so she moved to the edge of the tub towards him just as I done. Come here baby and let me help you then. Her was disappointed that it wasn't depth but she'd do for now. So he edged closer and she grabbed the towel away from him. His cock standing proud and ready. She reached out and turning to me said let momma take care of this, and bent forward taking his entire cock into her mouth.

He reaches to grab her hair and she quickly slaps his hands away as she pushes back. Gasping I've already had enough of your touching tonight. Her frowned and climbed into the tub. Now everyone relaxed back into their seats/ it was a fairly large hot tub so we had plenty of room. We actually had good conversations. Talked about things we had done growing up and the experiences we each had in out won ways. It was a beautiful night and I was floating away as I sat looking up into the night sky while they talked and laughed.

I should have been a Pisces instead of and Aries. I loved the water. Loved being in it. On it or around or even near it. Closing my eyes I could almost feel like I was floating in the ocean. The rhythm of the waves rocking me back and forth. Gawd I missed that. I could imagine quite nights with her in this tub. How erotic that could have been. I felt someone move up next to me it brought me back. I opened my eyes to feel her moving against me. Hey we thought we lost you, you got so quiet.

I looked into a pair of the most sensual eyes that I had ever seen. I knew she was in her mode now and just sat back ready to enjoy. One of her arms wen around my shoulders and the other across my chest. All this was under the water but it wouldn't have mattered.

I glanced over and could see Beth sitting talking with her husband. She was carefully mobbing closer and closer to her. In the meantime, she quickly slid around across my body until she was straddling me. My care cock rubbing across her silky mound. I didn't feel her bottom and look curiously into her eyes.

Smiling she said, momma took care of that baby, and raised her hand showing me the pieces of string that were her bottoms. She tossed them towards the table and then grabbed my head. Slowly leaning sown she acted like she was going to kiss me but at the last second turned and whispered in my ear its time baby. I am going to take Beth and him back into the play room, pretending to show him a cool way to get fucked. Of course he will be following wanting to do just that.

I want you to stay here. You will know when to come watch. She then reached behind her and untied her top; then tossing it towards her bottoms she raises up. She places both hands on either side of my head saying but first momma needs her baby to suck her tits. I sat still while she rubbed first one and the other across my lips. Come on baby suck them and I will fuck you good.

Her stiff nipples brushed across my lips and I wanted to so latch upon them until she screamed but for some reason I didn't think that's what she wanted.

Well fuck you then asshole she jumped up from me. Splashing around she grabbed Beth's hands and said come on you two. Beth I'll show you a cool way to get fucked. Beth turned to me asking what about you baby. I shrugged my shoulders saying I think I will just relax a bit more. You go on and have some fun. Her husband was about to cum thinking he was going to get some of Beth's fine ass.

She leads them back around the deck and into the play room. She and her husband were naked but Beth still had her little bikini on. once inside she showed them this large, what looked like a chair frame without a seat. She moved it out to the center of the room and asked Beth to come forward.

She did as she was directed and soon found herself on her hands and knees kind of tied to the frame. She then told her husband that he would have to get behind her and mount her. But he would also have to be tied to the frame that both of them being tied will make them move in unison with the frame and it's awesome.

Curiosity go the best of me and I climbed out of the tub and moved around through the house to the room. I came from a direction no one expected so they didn't notice me standing off to the side. At first I thought it was all up and up. Gawd Beth looked damn good on her hands and knees. I swear I could see her clit pressing through the tiny bottom and wanted to rip them off her to suck it. However the more I watched, I knew that he was too caught up in wanting to fuck Beth to realize the she was securing hiss to that frame.

I watched as she moved them into position. She then pulled the strings free on Beth bottoms and threw them across the room. Beth looked and up and she leaned down kissing her whispering just for a few minutes then you can pull free. Ok. Beth nodded ok and dropped her head. She then reached between them and guided her husband's cock to Beth's waiting pussy.

Her thrust forward and caught Beth by surprise. It had been early and hour and now the drugs we becoming more potent. Beth groaned oh yea fuck me slid that big dick deeper. Her tries to slide deeper but

SM GOLD

wasn't able to. He then tried to free himself of the frame and couldn't do that either. All this time she had moved around the wardrobe and picked up a ball gag. Moving back around quickly strapped it into his mouth.

He was shaking his head and muttering something all the while. Whispering into his ear she said fuck her baby. You wanted to fuck every time she comes over. You just want to fuck don't you baby.

All the while she is talking to him she is strapping on a huge fucking dildo. Once it's in place she steps back and takes a tube of lube, squirting it all along the shaft and then reaching sown and massaging it into his ass. His head is now whipping around trying to say stop I'm sure but the dumbass can't talk at all. I smile as I watch her now move behind her husband. She tells Beth you can get up now baby Beth slowly pulls free from her husband's cock, she then turns to him. Maybe I will get to fuck you after she does.

He's screaming into his gag now as she tells him. Baby I've waited so long to fuck you and with that she pushes the dildo. Against his ass. He tries to resist but soon she; sliding in and out. Then grabbing his hips she tells him damn baby you're tight hand on and slams the dildo as deep as it would go into his ass.

Beth gets up and goes to the wardrobe and takes a nice long vibrator. Then moving back in front of him, she lays down with her legs drawn up and begins masturbating in front of him while coaxing. Come on baby fuck him like you want to fuck me.

I stood watching the scene in front of me. I could see her from the side flexing her hips driving her big strap on cock deep in and out of her husband's poor ass. He was strapped to some sort of frame and unable to get away from her assault. In front of him lay Beth. Her tiny bikini gone now as she fucked herself with a vibrator and squeezed her big tits. She was screaming obscenities back. Make me cum and I might let you go. When I'm done with you. I don't want to ever see your sorry ass again and if I do ill slap you back down and fuck you till you can't walk.

12

Beth in the meantime was in her own little world. The ecstasy had sent her off into a pleasure filled trance. She lay withering through orgasm after orgasm begging to be fucked, come on baby forget him. He would have enjoyed the show. However it only made it feel that much less a man, here he was being brutally fucked while a hot babe was masturbating in front of him.

These three were in there own worlds. Looking around I see a clock and it's going on 2 in the morning. Suddenly the old man in me feels tired and I turn quietly around and move back to her bedroom. Pushing the door partially to. I climbed into her bed. I feel like I'm lost and the weight of the blankets seems to wrap me in warmth that comforts me, maybe it's her scent in them but whatever it is I soon fell fast asleep. I don't know why I don't fear they will come for me next. But I don't. I dream of a time sometime or another.

I can hear the sound of the surf. Can smell the salt in the air. The air is crisp and clear. The only sounds is the occasional shrieks of a gull or two and the waves washing ashore only to leave again. I'm lying in a hammock without a stich of clothes on. I'm not old anymore. There a sound and I look around to see her walking toward me.my gawd she is so beautiful her eyes are filled with life and excitement.

Her lips curled in an innocent smile. Her hair lightly blowing in the breeze. Her body, my gawd she is naked as the day she was born. Her tits bouncing and giggling with every step. She reaches me and moves into the hammock. She lays across me asking me why I am smiling. I could only answer I've never been so happy. We lay together watching the clouds pass over head without a care in the world.

I feel the bed move and start to wake. She slips beneath the covers with me and presses her naked body to mine. Tenderly running her fingers across my forehead and down over my lips.my eyes flutter open as she leans down and kisses me tenderly. I close my eyes enjoying the intimate touch. I've been looking for you. I was afraid you left.

You told me not to interfere so I didn't. Besides you looked to be enjoying yourself. Oh gawd that was hot. Now I understand why men act the way they do when they are fucking, it's so hot. I laughed saying well that interesting.

She lays her head on my chest and runs her hand down gently caressing my thick cock, no baby what I mean is, there is such a feeling of power. Gripping his hips and slamming that dick into him. I just can't imagine what it would feel like on your dick. I groaned as now she had me completely hard again. Did you stay long enough to watch me fuck Beth? No I missed that one. You would have liked that I bet.

Did Beth fuck your husband to? Laughing she looked into my eyes, she is fucking him now. When she is done, I'll let him go and he will get dressed, grab his shit and leave. I frowned that is her husband she is talking about. Leave where's he going to go? She sits up saying I don't give a shit but I'm tired of being the one to support his ass and him not doing a darn thing.

So baby she is done she want to be with me but she want to be with me alone. I looked at her saying ok. You'll have to go downstairs and occupy yourself but don't leave ok. Promise me you won't leave. Oh shit I'm sorry I forgot where I was for a minute there. Sure I'll get up and go downstairs and let you have some privacy with Beth.

She quickly moved across me. Straddling me and reaching down between us guilds my cock in her waiting pussy slowly she sinks down until she has me buried deep. Hmmmm I want more of this. I reached up to cup her tits bringing a nipple to my lips and sucking causing her to grind harder against me. Oh gawd you fucker you are trying to make me ruin the bed. Oh please no stop wait ....harder. She just as quickly pushes off me saying. Oh my gawd that was close.

How can you do that to me? I laughed shrugging my shoulders as I throw the sheets back and sit on the side of the bed. She gets up and moves to the door turning, now you promise not to leave. I promised.

She turned and headed back down the hall. Eventually the door had been closed because when she opened it I could hear him wailing and begging.

I got up pulled my jeans back on and a shirt. Then I headed down stairs to do some exploring. I walked into the den and first looked at the music collection. I saw some cd's I liked loaded them up and hit play. Next I walked into the kitchen and checked things out.

Nice very nice. Then I heard a mutter shouting. Then the upstairs door opened and I could hear the fight. She was screaming at him. Take your sorry ass back to where you came from. He was yelling you raped me bitch. She was laughing hell yea I did and I got it on tape so unless you want everyone to see you taking that big dick, you better take your ass out of here and don't come back. That did it for him and he stomped down stairs and into the guest bedroom. I took him a few minutes but soon he came out with a bag stuffed with shit and left. I shook my head at the turn of events. Not what I had expected to happen, not at all. Oh well sometimes things work and sometimes they don't. Turning around I find Beth standing in the doorway. She asked me to make sure you were still here. I smiled saying yep still here. She slowly walked toward me her big tits softly jiggling with each step.

Her nipples very stiff looked heavy. as she reached me she snaked her arms around my waist pressing those hug tits against me. I reached up and brushed a strand of hair from her eyes asking. Did you have fun? She looked away and then down saying no, not really. I thought it would be fun raping him but it wasn't what I wanted to do.

This puzzled me so I asked then why did you do it, she pulled me closer one day I came over but she wasn't home,he raped me. I hugged her close kissing her head saying its ok Beth. It's over now she looked up and I leaned down kissing her. She responded immediately wrapping her body around mine. Gawd this lady was hot, I broke the kiss reluctantly asking she's waiting upstairs for you.

I know but I want you to no something too. With that she took my hand in hers and slid it between us. Down her body and between her open legs.my fingers brushed across her swollen clit. Her whole body jerked and she looked into my eyes.my husband hates it and says I'm a freak.my fingers slowly wraparound it and I stroke it gently causing her to push away from me and spread her legs even more. Sensing what she wanted I dropped to my knees and begin kissing her swollen nub.

Her hands grab my head asking you don't think I'm a freak do you? I looked up into her eyes saying no I think you are wondering and wrapped my lips around her clit flicking my tongue across it.

She tries to pull away but I stay with her causing her to cry oh gawd no you are going to make me cum, suddenly there was a rush of cum across my mouth and splashing across the floor...her whole body was convulsing as she rode the orgasm. I released her clit and held her tightly as she panted, oh my gawd that has never happened. I'm so sorry.

I stood up and she blushes, you are soaked I smiled saying yea you squirted a lot, your special. She raised up on her toes and kissed me, then turned walking through the doorway, stopping she asked do you want to come with me? I smiled saying thank you but you go and enjoy yourselves

I'll be up later, you promise, what's with all the promises she smiles and heads out of the room. I leaned back against the counter thank you ecstasy holly shit that bed better have rubber sheets with those two. Wow! Was all I could say?

Beth was one hot number for sure and evidently she has some loser of a husband too. Look out buddy you'll find yourself at a party getting that ass pumped. I then grabbed some paper towels and cleaned up her mess from the floor. Shaking my head she had a basement. trying the door I see sure enough steps leading downstairs.

Turning on the lights I make my way down to find a larger room. It's got a pool table at one end and a sitting area at the other. smiling I see a stripper pole over to the side I remember her telling me stories of parties where she would be noticed into showing some of her old skills. She had told me that she was a dancer for a while but that she retired. Seeing her move I could believe it but now glancing across the walls I see old pics of her on stage. Gawd she looked just like in my dreams.

Noticing a huge TV I find the remote and cut it on. The screen comes to life but it's not TV. I look at the pictures and realize it's the play room. Looking around I see the vid recorder still running. I push the stop button on it and then see another box different buttons on it. Pushing one button changes to the den. Another to the deck. Another outside the front door, another outside the back door.

The last was the one I was looking for her room. Beth had just walked back into the bedroom. She was already in the bed and told Beth to crawl in. Beth was holding something behind her back and as she passed the camera I saw it was a huge strap on. Oh this was going to be good. I got up went upstairs made myself another drink and came back down just in time to see then moving around into a 69 position.

Something strange was happening, I would have thought she would be the dominant role but it looked and sounded a little like Beth was assuming that role. Beth was on top telling her suck it you bitch, suck my dick, all I could hear from her was some mumbling because evidently Beth had her pussy planted in her mouth.

I reached down and squeezed my cock watching those big tits on the girls. Beth then rolled off her and before she could get back on, she had moved around on the bed. If I didn't know better she was positioning herself better so the camera could she have known I would be here? Beth then moves around and lays across her.

Now they were kissing and feeling each other up. Beth raised up and squeezes her tits and rubbing hers against them asking. He likes big tits doesn't he? Who she answered Beth pins her arms down with her legs and slaps her across the face you know who bitch.

Yes he likes big tits this seems to please Beth as she sits up squeezing her own tits hard causing her nipples to jut out more. He's wanting mine. No Beth please Beth reaches down and slaps her again. Shut the fuck up bitch if I want him I'm going to have him. Raising up a little Beth scoots forward and grabbing her head says, suck my little dick bitch suck it good and I'll strap my big dick on and fuck you.

I watch as she takes Beth's little dick into her mouth and proceeds to suck, kiss and caress it. Beth is squeezing and pinching her nipples the whole time with her head thrown back is he a good fuck Beth asked? She finds her strength and rolls Beth off her saying stop it Beth. Why you don't want him. You broke the trust when you fucked bill. You tricked me Beth you know it.

I just have to explain it to him. Beth moved off the bed and began strapping on the huge dick bitch it doesn't matter you broke the trust and the collar is cut.no Beth it does matter she was watching Beth the whole time memorized by the huge dick on the big tit slut, now get over here I'm ready to fuck you. I couldn't believe what I was hearing. was this the same timid lady in the kitchen. Wow she was good. She was playing everyone well not everybody now,

Watching the screen I see her moving around the bed again. This time to give the perfect shot from behind Beth as she fucks her. Beth moves around between her legs and raises them then taking the huge rubber dick she rubs it across her slit causing her body to jerk. Oh gawd fuck me slam it in, gawd damn it.

Beth pushed forward driving about half the dick into her oh gawd that's big don't stop she cried Beth reaches up and grabs her nipples pulling roughly on them asking does it feel better then him bitch? He can't fuck you the way I can I watch as she works the rest of the rubber dick into her. Then the fucking starts Beth is slamming the big dick in her and her screaming oh gawd yes fuck me I'm your master you can fuck me whenever you want.

Beth just kept driving into her growling damn straight I can bitch. You're mine now. I'm going to put my collar on you tomorrow. I'm going to fuck you till you pass out. Then I'm going downstairs and I'm going to fuck him till I pass out. This sent her over the cliff and I can see squirt after long squirt splashing against Beth as she laughs "cum for me bitch, cum for me". Beth keeps pumping against her until she stops moving. Beth pulls the long dick from her abused cunt and sits back. She had finally passed out.

13

Beth stands up, unstraps the cock and drops it. She then flips the sheets over her and moves to the bathroom. I watched the bed, but she wasn't moving. I was beginning to get concerned when I noticed she rolled over and curled up under the covers. She was out that's for sure. Looking at the clock I see it is close to 4 in the morning now so she ought to be crashing. What about Beth though?

A few minutes later I watched her come out of the bathroom and go into her closet. She comes out a few minutes later dressed in a stunning white number with white stockings and heals. Standing in front of the mirror she fixes her hair and squeezing her big tits saying, 'Baby hope you're ready because there's a fucking coming your way." She then turns and heads out of the room.

I quickly turn the TV back to real TV and move over to the pool table. I started shooting around on it when I heard the click clack of her heals walking through the house. I smiled "she is looking for little old me". I left the door open in the basement and she found it. I bent over the table lining up a shot when I heard the click clack down the stairs.

Turning around I feel my cock leap in my jeans. Holy fuck she is hot. She smiles when she sees my eyes come back up to her body to her eyes. "Hi, you didn't leave". "I promised". Waving towards upstairs she says "she passed out so looks like it's just us now". "Well its getting late, we probably should call it a night too". "Oh, hell no, we aren't calling it a night" she thought.

"Could we just shoot a couple of games first and let me wind down". "Sure I'll rack them' I say as I grin "I'd like to get at that rack" I thought.

I set the game and she breaks. I almost came in my fucking jeans watching those big tits sway as she broke. Those watching her walk around the table had my tongue hanging out before the end of the first game. She was enjoying teasing me and I was enjoying allowing her to.

Walking up to me, she pressed herself against me saying "my husband like to take me out and show me off to men. He lets me dance with them and they feel me up while he watches. He won't let them fuck me though" and she moves away to take her shot." Oh God she's told her too much about me. She knows exactly what to say to get my attention" I thought. She missed her shot and she pouted saying "I just can't sink any balls tonight. L laughed saying" Oh, I bet you could".

Shyly looking back to me she says "what did you say?" "Nothing". "Hmmmm would you mind if we sit and just watch some TV. My feet are starting to hurt in these shoes and I'm getting tired". "No that's fine. Come on." I walk over to the large couch and crawl up into it. She follows behind me but gawd what a show it was. Those big tits swaying as she crawled towards me on her hands and knees. Then reaching me, flipping around and sitting up.

She brought a foot towards me asking me "would you take them off for me?"

I smile and reach for her foot. I slip the first shoe off and toss it to the floor. She then raises the other foot. As I reach for it I glance up and see she is wearing a tiny red thong and it is soaked. She smiles at me and runs a hand down and then runs a finger across her panties. I manage to slip the last shoe off. Tossing it to the floor as she ask "would you like a taste". She then pulls aside the tiny thong and I can see her wet swollen open pussy. Her clit standing hard and proud.

"Do you like my little dickey" she asks.

I reach over a grab a pillow and tell her "Raise your ass" I then start kissing up her nylon covered leg. Taking my time was driving her crazy or at least it sounded like it. "Oh gawd yes. Come eat momma's pussy baby. Come on baby its waiting. You know you want it. Come get it baby." I couldn't tell if this was still and act or not, but knew in a few minutes I'd have my answer. I reached that panty covered cunt. Carefully I kissed her panty covered clit and then quickly moved back down to start up her other leg.

As I make my way along I ask her "do you like putting on the show for your husband?" Oh gawd that feel so nice. What? Oh well yes it's nice to be noticed by men. I'm not as young as I was". I reached for her panties again and once again kissed her panty covered clit. Now I focused on kissing the skin at the edge of the thong.

All around it and soon it was soaked through. Her hips are jerking wildly every time I get near her clit. I run my hands up and wrapping my fingers through the thong I jerk and rip it from her body. She screams "gawd damn baby, eat momma's cunt. Come on baby make her cum" I roll over pulling her with me until now my head is on the pillow and I pull her forward until she is straddling my mouth.

I run my tongue deep into her pussy and flick it several times. Then moving slowly and firmly up till it's under her huge clit. "Oh gawd, no baby, not mommas little dickey baby, no it's too sensitive" As she is talking I'm gently wrapping my arms around her hips holding her firmly. "No baby, you can't, momma might make a MESSSSSSS" was all she got out as I took her clit between my lips and sucked.

She was covering me with her cum until I released her clit and went back to tonguing her pussy. Slipping it in and out and around, but not touching her clit. I relaxed my grip on her hips too.

She was panting now "oh gawd baby that was intense, but you can't do that anymore now. Mamma can't take that" I looked up and she was slumped forward and trying to sit back up. Her big tits were heaving with each breath. 'Fuck, you've got to be gentle with mamma's little dickey baby" I then began increasing my grip on her again and this signaled my pending attack. "NO NO NO please NOOOOOOO" as I once again took that hard clit between my lips sucking. Once again she covered me with her juices before I released her clit and started tonguing her again.

I released her grip on her hips and she groaned "Son of a bitch No you can't do that to mamma" She was gasping for breaths now and slumped back forward. Slowly sitting up she reached down and ran her hands through my hair saying "Oh baby mamma little dickey can't take any more. Come up her and let her take care of you" I slowly began increasing my grip again as she started wailing "no, no, I can't take it, please, no" as I began flicking my tongue hard across her clit and finally taking it between my lips sucking.

She went off like a rocket again this time reaching down trying to pry me from her as she screamed "Mother fucker you are killing me, Please, No, I'll do anything you want, but no more" I was covered again as I released her and went back to my gentle caresses. She tried to squirm free but I held her right where we were.

Finally making it to where she is sitting up again she looks down asking "baby you better be ready to fuck when you finish with me because you are driving me crazy, but you have to stop now. Please" as I attacked her again quickly. Leaving her humping her pussy to my mouth as she soaked me again. Releasing her this time, she rolls free panting and moving off the couch.

Gasping she cries "You son of a bitch. Stay away from me. You can't do that to me." She glances and sees that my cock is running down my thigh. My jeans wet were the tip has been leaking pre cum. "Oh shit, if I let you fuck me you've got to do it my way". "I don't like people taking control". "My husband thinks he has control but he doesn't"

I move off the couch, making sure I'm between her and the stairs. I strip off my soaked shirt and then peel off my jeans. She's still panting as she watches me. Then I begin moving towards her. "Now wait a minute, you have to let me control this. You can't keep doing what you've been doing to me". "Why not?" "Because I don't like it'. "It sure felt like you liked it. Look at those big nipples nice and hard. Momma's little dickey nice and hard. She's ready for a good fucking."

She was backing away from me holding her hands out. "Wait, gawd damn it". With a sigh I say "OK" but she relaxes" good now give me a minute" and drops her hands. As she does, I reach out grabbing her and pushing her face down into the couch. I then quickly move behind her and shove my stiff cock deep in her hot pussy. She struggles "holly shit, stop, oh gawd, not like this, stop, please, stop." As I'm fucking her I reach around under her. She realizing what I'm after grabs at my arm trying to keep me from reaching her. I do though and reaching her clit I pinch the hell out of it causing her to scream "NO" as she soaked the couch yet again. She's panting and screaming in the coach pillows as I continue sticking my cock in and out of that tight hot pussy.

Pulling my hand out from beneath her lets her relax a little. I then open the back of her nightie and then pull it from her quivering body as she grabs at it trying to keep covered up. "Please, No, Please, no, you can't take me like this" I slap her sweet ass a couple times as she brings her hands around trying to cover it. I smile and quickly bring my hand back underneath her as she screams

THE RELEASE

'OH NOOOOOO' as once again I pinch the shit out of her sore and sensitive clit. I can feel the couch cushions now soaked as I pull away from her. Leaving her panting a cussing as she rolls over "You sorry asshole. How dare you treat me like this? You're no better than my husband"

She stops talking as she looks into my eyes. Oh no, no, you can't be serious"......oh gawd no. you can't be serious, she threatened as she tried to stand up. I was standing

With my hard cock pointing toward her, till wet from the hot pussy, her big tit were heaving up and down s she panted. You haven't cum yet? She asked amazed that I was still hard. No were just getting started good. Oh hell no we aren't" she growled as she scooted forward on the couch. He legs draping over the edge and just touching the floor when I move forward again, her hands shoot out trying to push me away as she tells me No.

I'm done damn it no man treats me like this I'm too big and strong for this and soon I'm brushing up against those big tits. His hands now on my shoulders hitting me begging no oh please gawd no I can't take any more. I reached down and lift her legs up, which opens he pussy to my invading cock. I start sliding into that tight wet cunt as she falls back into the couch screaming you asshole ok then fuck me if you want to but I'm not going to enjoy it.

I continue forward until I'm buried once again. Then I release her legs and they fall to the side spread wide. Raising up on my hands I looked down at her. Holding my cock deep in her, I flex my hips causing my cock to raise up and stroke that big hot cum button of hers.

Her eyes were wide with trying to keep from letting me know what was happening to her I smiled and dropped my head to quickly wrap my lips around one of those huge nipples id been dying to suck on.as I take it between my lips and nibble against it, Her hands reach out trying to once again push me away. Oh fuck no you don't get to do that you asshole" I continued sucking and biting as her hands slowly stopped hitting my shoulders.

I could feel her hips begin to push with my grind against her cum button.no no gawd stop she screamed as she realized she was fast approaching another orgasm.it hit her quick as she suddenly started falling away beneath me, fuck, fuck, gawd harder you bastard fuck me harder"

I released her nipple and her hands shoot around grabbing my head and pushing it to the other nipple" suck it baby mommas going to cum, oh gawd you son of a bitch" I closed my teeth around her nipple as I felt the rush of her cumin. flooding my cock with her cum as her body thrashed beneath me leaving her once again gasping as I released her stiff nipple and move down her tit to leave a nice red mark. As my lips and teeth close into her tit flesh she screams oh gawd no, no, marks you can't but it was too late and I had a nice one on that tit. I intended to leave a few more before I was done.

I raised up and held still as she slowly relaxed through her bliss. Looking up at me through hooded eyes she groans "I'm a master damn it. You can't treat me like this." I smile down at her, sliding my cock slowly out until the head is at her entrance. "It's about time you realize who I am you fucking animal." I snarled down at her "I know exactly what the fuck you are" and slam my cock deep into her quivering cunt. She screams and starts hitting at my face. "No, no more, I won't let you fuck me this way."

I continued fucking her and as I did I left 4 big bite marks on those big tits. Her hands pushing and slapping at my head as I assaulted those big tits. "You asshole, my husband will see them. Stop, oh gawd, why, please stop". I don't care and it was my intention to leave her marked so her husband would know what a cunt she was. Lifting up again. I slipped my hands beneath her legs and lifted them up, pushing them against her chest with them hanging over my shoulders. She was too week at this point to fight much but still continued her verbal threats.

14

"**I** swear to gawd I will get even with you for this. STOP" as I pounded her abused cunt. Her head was trashing side to side screaming "No, No, No, I won't cum again you fucking jerk. I promise you that you won't get that satisfaction again."

I raised up off her and grabbed her feet with one hand holding them up against her big tits. "You won't cum again for me" "No, no more, you can't make me you bastard." Looking down to where my cock was sliding in and out between those swollen lips of her pussy, I ran my hand down to her stomach.

"Oh gawd, no, no, don't fucking touch me" she realized that she had no control and if I pushed that cum button again she wouldn't be able to stop. Her hands shot down and around trying to grab my hands, but she couldn't. My fingers moved down until I grab the base of that huge cum button. She stops moving at that point and her breath is coming in short gasps as she tries another tactic. "OK, OK, let me up and I will fuck you till you cum, but you can't touch me there. I'll be good to you, baby, cum for mamma."

I can feel her clit throbbing between my fingers as I continue stroking it. "Hmmm mommas big cum button is ready to be pushed "Her eyes widen in horror as she screams "Please, no," as my fingers close around the nub squeezing it.

Her body goes off again and hips begin fucking my cock. Sliding it in and out as I squeeze and stroke her clit. Her ejaculations are getting less but it's the response of her body that rocks her. I release her button and she continues fucking me for a few more minutes before her legs and arms fall to her sides as she gasps "You are a son of a bitch, why are you doing this to me."

Looking down at her I tell her "I watched you fuck her upstairs just now. I saw how you degraded her and then brutally fucked her to your pleasure. Giving no sense of what it must have felt like to her. It was just about your pleasure". Her eyes widened, "how" I pulled free from her still quivering cunt and walked over to the TV, pushing the button bringing the picture of her bedroom on the screen.

She lays back. "You watched us?" I turned and walked back towards the couch. She is laying back, her big tits heaving and her legs still spread wide revealing her open and fucked pussy. Her eyes look down at my bouncing cock and she shudders "oh gawd, no more, you still haven't cum" She quickly closes her legs as I stand before her "how does it feel to be used for someone else pleasure?" Her eyes look down and then back at me "well I can't lie and say I haven't enjoyed it, but get to the point" Struggling to lift up she reaches out a hand asking "help me up now please."

I knew that she hadn't learned her lesson yet and slapped her hand away causing her to fall to one side. As she did, she effectively rolled over onto her hands and knees. I quickly move up grabbing her hips, shove my cock back into that hot pussy. "OHHH gawd no more. I swear I will treat her better" I grinned "Oh you sweet little slut. I've got one more fuck for you".

"Shit you bastard, get it over with" and she began rocking her hips. Taking me deep and then back out and then back in. She knew that this way I wouldn't have contact with her clit and all she had to do was not let my hands under her. She was concentrating on that as I grabbed her hips and pumped into her.

"Oh yea, now he'll cum" she thought. I was spreading her ass open as she rocked forward and watching that sweet little asshole flex with each thrust. "Oh yea baby. This feels so good" I groan. "Yea baby, like that, momma likes that. Cum for me baby, fill me with it. I want to feel you coming" she coaxed. Finally I groaned "ready momma" She wanted me to finish and be done with me. "Yea baby, let me do it" As she began rocking back and forth faster.

I was ready, spreading her ass as she rocked forward I slipped from her pussy and planted my cock at her ass and as she rocked back I slid deep into her ass. She hadn't expected that and was rocking too hard to stop and before she could fully react I was balls deep in her tight ass. "SHHIIIITTTTTT NOOOOO" she screamed as she tried to pull away from my cock. I was holding tight to her hips as she moved forward on the couch I moved with her until her head was buried against the back of the couch with no were to go.

"NOOOO, you are splitting me in two. NOOOOO gawd please take it out. I'll fuck you any way you want but not in my ass" she pleaded into the couch cushion. I didn't care, this was sweet. Her ass was flexing with each movement she made. I hadn't started fucking her yet, I was just holding myself buried in her. She must have passed out because she stopped screaming and I could feel her ass relaxing. I started slowly sliding in and out of her now. Sliding my whole cock out and then sliding it back in as I held her hips up. She was going to remember this night.

As her hands dropped, mine moved down and soon I had her cum button again between my fingers. As her body began thrashing beneath me as she screamed not again no I can't take it again, gawd you are going to tear it off, stop as I stroked her clit. I then squeezes her clit causing her to scoot forward on the couch screaming" fuck me harder fuck my ass harder" gawd I loved it when a women lets go and talked like this. I fucked her hard as she rode through another long orgasm.

As she fell forward I slipped from her ass as it milked my cock. She quickly rolled over not wanting to give me another chance at her ass. Her breathing was raging now and sweat had soaked her hair.

Breathing deeply did you enjoy your fuck asshole? I smiled and jumped up pinning her arms with my legs and now sitting on top of her chest. My wet cock laying between her big tits. Her eyes looked down you've got to be kidding me" you still haven't cum: she asked as I began to stroke my shit covered cock between her creamy tits.

Pushing forward the head reaches her lips and she tries to turn away but I reached down holding her head no baby. I'm going to cum" her eyes widen as she starts to say" I'm not going to suck your cock after its been in my ass" but as her mouth opens I push the head of my cock between her lips leaving her struggling to get it out. I can feel her tongue around the head trying to push it from her lips and smile down saying might as well relax its going to happen.

Grabbing a handful of her hair in one hand I reach the other behind me. Her eyes glare at me as she closes her legs trying to stop me. I just keep smiling as my fingers push between her wet thighs and reach her cum button.

This time as I squeezed it her mouth fell open and I shoved the rest of my cock into it. She begins sucking, as I blast my cum against the back of her throat.

She sucking my cock like a baby on its mother's nipple as her orgasm rages through her. Finally my spent cock slips from her lips and I roll off her. She struggles to sit up coughing and cussing me. I've never been treated like that ever you asshole. I was lying back catching my breath as she rolled over laying her head on my chest.

I've soaked this couch" she whispered as her head tenderly ran up and down my body. She was tenderly kissing my chest as I could feel her heavy breath against me. Her big tits brushing my thighs as she breathed.

I pushed her off me and stand up. I noticed its getting light outside, I picked my jeans and shirt up slipping them on. I need to get some rest" I say as I turn to see her still laid out on the couch. No matter how she screamed and cussed. I could tell she was very well satisfied I had to admit although the bitch was hot.

I pulled my phone out and took a picture of her laying there with her legs spread revealing her red swollen and abused cunt. Her clit still standing out and her big tits and nipples proudly on display. She tried to cover up as I took the picture but I got it before she did. Oh no you don't and rolled off the couch.

Looking around she says shit its late, he'll be home soon I've got to go" and turned heading up the stairs. I followed Beth upstairs planning my last act on her. Quietly moving into her room. Looking down she was sleeping so soundly, I write a note saying give me a call when you get going again" I got my bag, slipped my shoes on and went to find Beth. She was in the bathroom putting on some makeup. She was trying to cover up the huge hickey on her neck.

"You asshole" how am I going to explain this she had her jeans on but was still topless perfect.

Come on and I grabbed her by the arm pulling her out of the bathroom and through the room down the stairs and to the front door. Stop gawd damn it I don't have a top on yet" I sneer it doesn't matter, I'm taking you home".

What no I can drive myself I dragged her to my car, opened the door and shoved her in. she was struggling with her little halter top trying to get it in place as I jumped in and started the car. No you can't take me home my husband might be there. She stopped saying oh gawd that's what you wanted" I pull away and open my phone getting her address as I drive she is trying to get herself together.

We pull up in front of her house. She sighs as she doesn't see her husband's truck. He's not home yet so she's clear.

Smiling I reach over and with a jerk of my hand I rip her little halter top away from her body, leaving her heaving tits out in the open. What the fuck, screams as she tries to cover her big tits. I reach over and open her door saying get out. I then toss the halter out the door. She reluctantly steps out of my car and picks up the torn halter.

Her big tits have my bite marks all around them. Just then her husband pulls up in the drive way. Her eyes widen as she turns to me and I wave. Write if you ever want to do it again, and pulls away from the curb. The door slamming shut as I look in the rearview mirror. Her trying to cover her big tits as he walks up waving his arms around.

I drive on over to my hotel room, take a long shower and crawl into bed. I fall fast asleep and sleep until 6 or 7 that evening. Waking I see a text from her. Opening it I read: wow what a night. I don't remember a lot of it but what I do remember. WOW! Beth called and she's mad as a wet hen. She says you marked her up I asked her if her husband was mad.

She said no, that actually he had fucked her as soon as she got home. What did you do to her? I'm sorry about breaking our trust and I understand. I hope that you will come see me again sometime. Take care master.

I close my phone and drift back off to dream land. I was again at the beach. The air smelled of salt and water. The waves were reaching again for the shoreline. The sky was crystal clear and it was hard to tell where the water ended and the sky begin. I was laying in my hammock stroking my cock. Looking over I see a woman approaching me.

I don't recognize her though but admire her beauty... and I think about all the fun I had just had and I smile. I no longer had a sub and I was already missing that hmmmm... even a Dom doesn't feel whole without a sub as a sub doesn't feel whole without a Dom.

So he secedes to see if he can find one when evening hit he went to the bar at the hotel just to see what was going on and on the dance floor he sees the salute of a lady when the music stopped he realizes it was the female that was coming toward him at the beach, she was wildly beautiful but yet had a look of want in her eyes like if she was looking something. Hmmmm. Could this be who I'm looking for so I stood up and walked toward her hello he says can I buy you a drink she looks up at him and says yes please but you can also buy me. He said oh I'm sorry you looked a little lost or something I just wanted to see if I could help.

She smiled actually you can I hope. What the problem, well it's like this I work here as I said before and well don't get me wrong I enjoy what I do and the money is great but he looked into her eyes and said but what?

Never mind you wouldn't understand, you don't even know me. I can't possibly get into this with you try me he said how about I tell you a little about me first. She smiled again and ok. Well ok then I'm what's known as a Dom.

I do understand more than you think she looked at him and explain please. I've been in the BD/SM lifestyle for most of all life. I have had many subs with many problems from everyday problems to sexual ones so please what's wrong? She paused for a minute and will again I enjoy my job.

I enjoy sleeping with men and even females, but I can't let go I don't know what to expect and I don't want to embarrasses myself either so I stop before I enjoy my job, I enjoy myself and well the more I think about it the ore I would like to without someone judging me. He smiled she said see you think this is a joke.

No he said quickly not at all I'm smiling because more than half the females in the world have the same problem and they have gotten used to just having orgasms that now it just seems normal for them but yet they feel like they are missing something.

He said actually I can help you with this but first I'd like to just talk with you and let you in on what the lifestyle is all about if that's ok with you.

She said ok but what will I owe you she was so used to owing people no one does anything for nothing. He said nothing again with being a Dom I enjoy seeing someone enjoy themselves and I love seeing them finally release and realize who they really are.

So tell me about you a little. What kinds of things do you enjoy sexually, like do you kike pain at all. Have you ever been tied up, do you like being told what to do? She looked at him and said wow there's a lot to this, it's not like you see in porn's at all she said no it's not.

A Dom learns there sub so that the sub can be the best they can be sexually and in everyday life as well one actually goes hand in hand with the other. They sat and talked for hours he finally said would you like to go back to my room I will pay you. I just would really not rather be alone tonight she smiled and said I would love to. They went back to the room.

What she didn't know he was actually missing his sub the last he had heard from her was the text saying Beth was mad because I left marks her. He looked at this girl he just brought back to his room and wondered if she could help him forget and if he could get her to play a little…He shut the door behind them and said so can I get your name she looked at him and well I don't normally tell that but there is something different about you my name is Donna. WOW! I don't believe I just told you that. He said. Well Donna I'm mike nice to meet you. Would you like to learn more about the lifestyle or no, it's up to you. Donna said sure it's very interesting, and not like I had heard of.

So mike said well sit down and I'll show you a few things and explain as we go ok, she said ok…. He grabbed his tote bag off the floor and unzipped it. He started pulling things out and laying them on the bed. Donna's eyes grew big what have I gotten myself into? Mike said don't worry, I won't do anything you don't want to ok…. He pulled out some restraints and said my I show you Donna, reluctantly said yes so he placed cuffs on her wrists and on her ankles. He said see there not so bad. She said no mike ok now one thing a Dom is good at is teaching their sub how to relax and let go so tell me more about you.

Do you like any kind of pain? Donna said well some not a lot though mike said ok. Do you like toys? Donna turned red and said yes, ok do you like blind folds? Donna said I've never had one. Mike said yes but you need to have a safe word a word that is used if something is hurting you and then everything stops. Donna said I understand. Mike said ok lay back on the bed and trust me, Donna was a little uncomfortable right now hell she thought I don't even know him, but yet there was something about him. A soft gentle side to him so she let him continue. About then mike reached over and grabbed a blindfold and leaned down and said trust me. I won't hurt you I'm just going to show you how to release ok. Donna quietly said ok.

Next he went into his bag and grabbed a head set and said I have some music I'd like you to listen to. It will help you relax ok. She said ok he put the head set on her and then programed his iPod it started to play. Very intense yet of music. Donna was relaxing she had seen the toys in his bag and on the bed and knew he was probably going to use them on her she tried to pre-pair her herself...

Mike started his finger up and down her lovely body not a flaw on it. She started to moan but didn't realize he could hear her because of the headsets. Mike knew she was relaxing he smiled and wondered how far he could take this stranger before she wanted to stop hmmmm.

Well now let's see.

He grabbed a vibrator and started running it up and down, all over her body as her body moved she as moaning so he ran it onto her clit. Her body jumped with surprise her smile was gone she knew she couldn't turn back now.

Mike started running his hand on her to relax her again and started kissing her neck and worked his way down to her nipples she was moaning his other hand started using the vibrator on her clit. She smiled, and was grinding her teeth. She didn't want him to know she was enjoying herself with her mouth closed she knew she wouldn't cum she could control her body very well. Mike reached down and got a bottle of lube and grabbed a bigger vibrator. Out of his bag and then grabbed a vibrator that he plugged in she hadn't seen this one yet.

He put lube on the large vibrator and turned it on and turned the other one on as well. He leaned over and took one of the earplugs out and said trust me, Donna I will not hurt you ok. Donna said ok so he placed the ear bud back into her ear he placed a pillow under her ass and started to insert the vibrato into he already wet pussy, which gave Mike a clue into what her she liked not knowing she jumped so he slowed down. Once he got the vibrator inside her she moaned.

He started pumping it in and out very fast her body started to move she was moaning and saying no stop, I can't do this. Mike continued this wasn't her safe word. He went faster and faster, harder and harder. Donna clenched her teeth mike reached up and opened her mouth and said breath baby breath. But every time he let her mouth go she clenched her teeth mike knew if she didn't breathe threw her mouth she wouldn't cum, she stopped and dug into his bag and pulled out a leather whip he put the handle of it in her mouth and then he started again, her hips started to move with every move he made with the toy.

She was so close, but she kept stopping so mike turned the plug in one on and placed it on her clit as he had the other insider her this took her to the next level she started to pant. Her body started to jerk. She was shaking her head no, mike didn't listen. He continued as he did. She came so hard the bed was soaked he continued to do it he had her cum 4 times and then stopped her body was alive. He took the ear buds out and took the blindfold off and smiled as he looked at her she closed her eyes she was embarrassed.

Mike reached up and took a firmer grip on her chin and said I said look at me she opened her eyes. He smiled and said there you ar.

That wasn't so bad was it? Donna shook her head no he began to run his hands up and down her body she liked how this felt omg. Please I don't think I can take it anymore. Mike said Donna remember I said I wouldn't hurt you, I want you to trust me baby girl.

He let her relax for about fifteen minutes and then asked her, do you want the blindfold and earbuds back on or would you like to see what I am going to do with you next?

She certainly was a stunning woman. If I had seen her on the street, I would have never guessed she was a hooker. Hell even in the club it didn't dawn on me. Still she wasn't in Beth's league but she was sweet. I had just watched her go through 3 or 4 intense orgasms and it surprised him to find yet another squirter. He was lucky to find one but to have found 3 in one weekend was something special.

Squirter's were special because they could reach a sexual peak that few women could or would allow themselves to reach. Most would feel rush but would hold it back and deny themselves that pleasure for feel of being embarrassed. Looking back to the woman before him he watched her breathing. Her eyes never really at him unless he commanded her to. He still didn't think she had it in her to be a complete sub. She was hiding something still. I asked her. Do you want the blind fold and earbuds or do you want to see what I'm doing. She hesitated for a few minutes as she looked from her body back to my eyes and back away.

Would you please release me? I had expected that. It was her way of seeing if she could trust me. Would I release her or would I continue on. I smiled saying of course, hang just a second and let me put this way. No you don't have to do that. Just let me up for a minute. I reached over and untied her legs and then stood up mobbing to the side of the bed.

As I untied one I noticed her turn and look at my crotch. She wanted to know if she excited me. She was used to men taking what they wanted from her. She excited them and she loved the feeling of being wanted. With me she didn't know and it unnerved her. I moved around to the other side and released that arm.

She slowly sat up in the bed rubbing her wrists. They got kind of tight there for a few minutes and shyly smiled. I haven with a few hookers in my life and they weren't shy in the least bit. Maybe on her usual terms she would be different but here with me she was on a different playing field. She got up and walked over to her bag, digging through it and finally standing up asking mind if I smoke I said, well I rather you step outside if you don't mind. She grinned saying ok I grinned saying I will be right back then, and slipped back into her dress. It clung to her body like a second skin. I watched as grabbed the bag and opened the door. She turned back towards me and smiled before closing the door.

I knew she wouldn't be coming back. I hadn't paid her yet so it was of no real loss to me. Still I wondered about her. There was something about her that I wanted to find out more. I sat a few minutes and then got up putting away my tools. I washed the vibrator and dried them. Then cut the TV on to watch something before dropping back off asleep. I went in and took a long hot shower. Then climbed into bed

Opening my phone I noticed I had two texts. One was from my previous sub. Opening it I read

Hi:

I was wondering if maybe we could get together tonight. You know just some dinner and talk. Well let me know.

I looked at the time it was sent and realized that I had missed it. I answered her:

Hi there

Sorry but I just got your text. I was out and met a very curious hooker at the club. Her name is Donna. You know her?

Then I opened the second text. It was from a number I didn't recognize and usually don't answer.

Hey asshole

Just thought I'd text you and tell you that my husband has been fucking me like a teenager. Seems those marks you left on me are driving him crazy. Still I want you to know that it was an incredible experience you put me through. I've never let anyone make me cum like that before or since.

Beth

I smiled and didn't respond. As I closed my phone I heard it beep. Another number I didn't recognize. Opening it I read:

Hi

It's me Donna. I snuck your number when you weren't looking. Sorry. I don't know how you did what you did but I haven't allowed that ever to happen. It scares me. Can I have some time to think?
I replied back: yes

I then closed my phone and sat back watching TV. I dosed for a few minutes and woke up to the beep of my phone. Gawd I've gotten awful popular I groaned.

Opening my phone I see a text from my ex sub.

Hey

Guess who is over here? Donna. She was telling me about this strange guy she met. How he was some sort of Dom or something. That she had agreed to meet with him and he had done something to her that has her shaken.

I texted back:

WOW!
Is she alright? She seemed fine when she left here.
Yes she's fine. She experienced something, as she put it, that she has never let anyone see.
Well good. Tell her I won't tell anybody.

LOL. If she agrees, would you come over here?

It's getting late.
Is that a No.?
I've got nowhere to be. Yea if you want. I can come by.
Ok hang on.
How do you know her?
We've been friends for a long time. I've wanted to be with her since I met her but I've been chicken. Beth intimidated me and I couldn't stop her. Donna though is different. Ok she says for you to come over. Ok on my way.

I slip my clothes on, grab my keys and head out the door. On my drive over, I wonder what's in store for me tonight. The last time I was over at her house, things got bent way out of shape. Plus I haven't had much time to divorce myself of her. I'd have to restrain from treating her like my sub. That's may be difficult. Then with Donna there, what was going through her head. She mentioned she had wanted to be with her since they met.

I drove up and climbed out of the rental car. Walking up to the front door. it opens and she steps out shutting it "I need to talk to you before you come in" ok, want to sit on the steps? I sit down and look up at her. She is wearing a long flowing silk robe. it clings to her body and leaves nothing to my imagination. Gawd she was hot. I tried to get my concentration back as she smiles" that's what I want to talk to you about" I laughed saying" sorry but you are a stunning women". She smiles "I know I screwed up our Dom/sub relationship but I will not let you go. I looked at her asking "what" I accept that you have released me from our bond as a Dom/sub, but I will not accept you walking out of my life. You mean too much to me."

I was touched and had to keep my wits here. Sweetheart, there is nothing I would like more than to stay a part of your life" she was in my lap in a flash, with her arms around my neck sharing a very, very, hot kiss. Pulling away from me looking into my eyes she purrs," I think we can come up with a new relationship that will be pleasurable to both of us." I smiled as my hands moved over her silk covered body" hmmmm I'm for that"

16

I'm glad you agree because now I have a surprise for you" I look puzzled, stand up she takes my hands saying "follow me" we are going to go to the guest room first and let you get changed. Turning as she entered the house and watched as I closed the door. She opens her robe. She's wearing a black latex dominatrix corset that ran from her luscious cleavage all the way down to her black stiletto heels. Damn you know how to get a man's attention" smiling she adds" and a women's.

My eyes narrow as she smiles. Come on time for you to get undressed and put your robe on "my robe" yes come on now. It's for effect" you know I don't wear costumes "listen when you were my master you got your way. Now we are equal and trust me, where the fucking robe and hood" "yes hood". Trust me baby, it needs to be this way" ok I'll try it your way this time.

Thanks baby as she slides up to me unbuttoning my shirt and pushing it from my shoulders. Then reaching down she unbuttons my jeans, rips down the zipper and pushes them off my hips. She then reaches down and grabs my hardening cock saying did you fuck her.

What" you heard me, did you fuck her? If you mean Donna no good because from now on baby this is mine and no one gets it until I say they can. Looking into her eyes I say "really" reaching up she takes the zipper in the front of her suit and slowly pulls it down revealing more and more of her body. And this is yours as she waits for my response. We tried that already, remember" baby I swear to you that it won't happen again. I was tricked but that was my fault.

I looked at her and gawd she looked good. Ok we can give it a try. She pressed her naked tits against my chest kissing me saying "you still haven't fucked me yet" I started to reach for her but she slipped from my grasp smiling" and you don't get to for a while yet" I groaned you tease" yes I am and you love it" now get dressed and meet me at the top of the stairs

I slipped the big black robe on and noticed it doesn't have any way of securing it closed.it would hang off my shoulders with my cock hanging in view. I shrug thinking she's nuts and then pull the hood over my head.

Looking into the mirror I see you can't see my facial featured beneath the huge hood. Laughing I step out of the room and to the stairs looking up I see her standing at the top. She has a riding crop in her hand swatting her thigh. Gawd my cock was at full attention already, smiling she says. I see you are up for the night activities" I looked down shrugging what I can say you're hot. Smiling she held out her hand"

I want us to walk holding hands I want to take the lead tonight ok you are my assistant.as you have probably guessed, Donna is waiting on the other side of the door. She has been prepared and has been waiting all this time very nice smiling she continues I learned from the best. Taking my hand she reaches out and opens the door and we walk in. there is soft jazz cd playing in the background and the room is lit by candles placed around it. I have to admit she knew how to make a production out of it.

I look to my right where she had hung the night before and the chains were empty. Then glancing to my left I see Donna secured to a large St. Andrews cross. There is a white silk sheet draped across her body covering her but her eyes are wide with both excitement and fear.

Who's that she whispered that's my assistant as she walks around the room in front of Donna. letting her see her and to make a statement. she was in control here. Looking over to me. She doesn't speak but I understand her gesture and move around the other side of the room to the wardrobe and stand still.

Donna's gaze leaves me as she hears her heels clicking across the floor toward her. Standing in front of Donna she spreads her legs and pushes her shoulders back giving Donna a delicious view. Donna you and I have been friends for a long time. yes we have. For tonight you are going to refer to me as mistress and I'm going to refer to you as my pet. Ok she slaps the crop against the padded bench causing a very loud slap.

What did you say oh yes mistress. Donna was almost stuttering and I wanted to suggest something not so fierce for her first time but she was the boss so I let it go hoping it would work out ok. Raising the crop, she trailed it across Donna's body. Donna's face was filled with fear as she slowly pushed the silk sheet away from Donna's body revealing the hookers lush frame. I almost groaned, but caught myself.

She then trailed the crop around Donna's neck and down across each of her swollen nipples. There she softly patted each one leaving Donna gasping. Standing back again, she reached up and pulled the zipper on her suit down. Revealing her creamy body beneath the black latex. "My pet, tonight you meet a man and you let him make you do what". Donna turned her eyes to me and then back to her. "Don't look at him. You answer to me. You let him make you do what". Donna didn't want to say it. She knew she didn't.

Raising the crop, she slowly circled a still nipple and then as quick as a humming bird's wing, she struck. Leaving Donna's nipple quivering from the blow and Donna screaming "Holly shit that hurt" Standing in front of Donna she stood tall waiting. Donna still hadn't answered when the next blow struck leaving Donna howling "Fuck, oh gawd, OK I've had enough".

She ran the crop around one of her big tits and slapped at the nipple "Tell me"

Taking a deep breath she began "OK, I met this guy and he talked me into being tied up. Kind of like this but on his bed. Anyway, he made me cum 4 times". I was listening and smiled knowing she had left something out. Did she know?

Slowly lowering the crop and running it between Donna's legs she asks "is that all". Donna was trying to get to toes and away from the crop before she answered. Did she know it was me standing there? I hadn't mentioned it in the texts so did she tell her Mistress? "Since you are pausing, I take it there's more". Donna tried to shake her head but before she could do it, she landed another blow but this one was on her inner thigh. Donna let loose a scream "Holly shit that hurt. OK I'm not into pain"

I cringed as I knew this was probably going to call for a strict punishment. Which it did and she delivered another sharp blow to the inner thigh. Donna yelped "Mistress, sorry Mistress, Please stop. I don't like pain" "How do you know what you like My Pet. You've allowed men to use you for their pleasure all these years. You don't know what you like." She then stepped closer to Donna and taking her hand she moved it between Donna's spread legs. Donna looked down watching, horrified at what might happen next. She ran her fingers through Donna's mound and brought them up to her nose. Sniffing them she smiled saying "Looks to me you do like a little pain".

Donna's eyes were wide and her mouth hung open as she realized, she was right. Her pussy was on fire and her clit was throbbing. She groaned "oh Mistress, when I came I squirted". Her eyes closed as if she was ashamed of it. Her head turned towards me and her eyes were a fire as she started walking towards me. HMMMMM. This is interesting I thought. When she reached me she whispered "she squirts". I smile saying "just like you mistress". I could see her chest rising and falling faster and I bet if I had ran my fingers sown between her legs I would have found her soaked. "You might tone it down just a little for her first time, ok". She looked back into my eyes whispering "oh ok, I guess I was getting a little carried away".

Yeah we don't want her running from the house screaming help, help, and help. She wanted to bust out laughing but held it in as she turned back to Donna.

She moved slowly and seductively to her pet. Moving right up against she purred into Donna's ear Hmmm you tasted good, and bent down biting Donna's neck. Donna was struggling to get free from her ties and she moved her hands all over her body. Squeezing her big tits, rolling her stiff nipples and then opening her pussy lips to stoke her fingers through them. Donna was going nuts "oh gawd Mistress, what are you doing to me." Slowly stepping back she peeled one of her big tits from her suit, revealing her swollen stiff nipple.

Then stepping up, held it to Donna's lips, "suck it My Pet". Donna quickly wrapped her lips around it sucking it like a baby to its mother's tit/ Reluctantly stepping back she signals me forward. Watching the two of them had given me such a hard on and now standing beside her facing Donna it pointed at what it wanted. Donna looked down at my cock and I watched as her tongue slipped across her lips. "Sorry My Pet but that is mine, I will let you enjoy something else though, but first you have to be blindfolded". Donna cut her eyes from my cock back to her Mistress and then said, "Ok Mistress".

Julie grabbed my sleeve and turned walking to the wardrobe. I followed her enjoying that sweet ass as it wiggled. Once at the wardrobe I picked up a blind fold and handed it to her. She turned and walked over to Donna. Very slowly she raised her hand and slipped the blindfold over her eyes. Then leaning forward, kissed her tenderly. I'm going to get somethings ready. My assistant will bring you to me. Donna was breathing in deep gasps as she responded, "Yes Mistress".

Julie then turned and walked back over to me. Reaching down and gently stroking my hard cock she whispers, "I'm going to need you to let me do somethings. Ok". Sure, it's your show Mistress. She squeezed my cock with that saying, "I like this new relationship". Take her down and bring her to my room. Yes Mistress, I groan. Softly pulling on my cock she leans forward and gives me a very, very hot kiss saying, "HMMM I'm going to take good care of this."

Then she turned and left the room. I looked over to Donna and watched her for a moment. Then selecting a waist belt from the wardrobe I walk over to her. I'm going to put a belt around your waist. It has loops on it that I will be attaching your wrist too. Yes, and she paused. You may call me Sir. Yes Sir. I then carefully attached the belt to her waist. Then I released one hand and attached it to the belt. Then the next. Sir do I know you, your voice sounds familiar.

I smile, no you don't know me. I then released her ankles. I let her stand for a minute moving her legs back and forth. The first time on the cross can leave you a bit sore.

I then lead her out of the play room, down the hall and into Julie's room. She came out of the closet with several large silk sheets. She then threw them over the rubber sheet on the bed. Oh she's expecting a mess, I smiled. Julie then looked towards me. My Pet, I want you to remain still. Yes Mistress. Julie then reaches out for my hand. Curiously I gave her my hand and she leads me to the foot of the bed there she pulls me close whispering, ok baby, this is where you will have to trust me. I look into those mischievous eyes, "ok". She then produces two cuffs. I raise my hands and she quickly wraps them around my waist. She then jumps up on the bed at the foot and signals me forward. Drop the robe, she instructs. I do as she asks and drop the robe. She smiles, hmmmm, this is going to be fun she whispers.

I don't know what she has in mind but hey I like an adventure. She holds her hand out and I give her mine. Raising it she connects it to the chain from the ceiling. Then she does the other hand leaving me now standing naked at the foot of the bed with my hands suspended over my head. My cock starting to lose its thickness as a bit of wonder enters my mind. I had witnessed her totally abusing her ex-husband last night and couldn't help but wonder what was in store for me.

Quickly moving off the bed she says be patient my pet, almost ready. She then moves back over behind me running her hands over my body. HMMMMMM, I think I could get used to you being here. I groan, Yes Mistress she wiggles against my back, letting me feel her tits rubbing against me, "good Boy". Momma is going to give you a treat later. Now baby, when I say I've always wanted the best of both worlds, I want you to shove this big beautiful cock in my hot wet pussy. So pay attention remember, I've always wanted both worlds. Yes Mistress.

Julie then moves back to Donna. Now My Pet, I'm going to lay you on my bed. Then I'm going to secure your hands and ankles again. Yes Mistress. I watched the two of these gorgeous women moving before me. Julie then carefully laid Donna on the bed with her head at the foot of the bet. Julie was careful to scoot her back in front of me. If she raises up, she would find my hanging cock.

I smiled at Julie as she secured Donna to her bed. Once secured, she gets up and turns some music on. Then diming the lights she lights some candles. She then stands where I can see her and she drops the robe from her shoulders revealing her naked body. My cock bounces and she smiles putting p finger to her lips.

17

I watch as she crawls on the bed, and lays face to face with Donna. She begins softly kissing her neck and whispering to Donna, I've always wanted to do this. Donna tried to turn her head to Julie but she wouldn't her. Looking up at me, she slips Donna's blindfold from her eyes.

It takes her a few moments for her eyes to adjust but she quickly sees a hard cock just above her. Julie rolls over to Donna's side and reaches up letting her fingers just barely touch my balls. HMMM nice isn't it. Donna looked from my cock back to Julie, "Yes Mistress". Julie let her fingers continue up the underside of my cock as her hand cupped and squeezed Donna's big tit. Oh gawd Mistress, Donna moaned.

Oh look My Pet. Donna looked to where Julie was looking and gasp as she sees a large drop of clear thick pre-cum ready to drip from my cock. Julie then said, "Close your mouth My Pet". Donna closed her mouth and Julie brings my cock down and rubs the pre-cum across Donna's lips. She then releases me and quickly takes Donna's lips into hers sharing a long and very sexy kiss.

I'm hanging there watching these two goddess below me and wonder what my Mistress might have in store for me. Julie kept kissing Donna and letting her hands stroke her shoulders and tenderly moving down cupping both heaving tits. Julie finally released Donna's lips leaving both gasping as Julie squeezed her tits. Then looking into Donna's eyes she slowly bends down and begins licking Donna's stiff nipples. Donna tries to thrash around which one, only causes her to bump my hard cock above her.

Laying back down now as Julie continues teasing her nipples, she raises her head and lets her tongue tickle my hanging balls.

I groan, Holy fuck which causes Julie to look up. HMMMM. You're being naughty my pet. Donna dropped her head back sown saying "Sorry Mistress".

Julie smiles up to me saying its ok My Pet, that's why he is there. I can see how excited he is, but I can't see how excited you are. As she was saying this, her fingers released Donna's tits and started slowly down her body. Donna arched her back as Julie's fingers slipped between her legs. HMMM My Pet is very wet, and slowly ran her fingers over her mound. In the meantime Donna had raised back up and was tickling my balls again with her tongue.

Julie then began kissing her way down Donna's body. Once again this caused Donna to drop her head back down and arch her back squealing oh gawd Mistress, don't make me, please I can't. Julie didn't listen and kept right on kissing until she was laying between Donna's legs. Donna raised her head up to look down to see what she was doing, but when she did, my cock was laid against her cheek.

Now I could feel her gasping breath as we both watched Julie begin kissing Donna's mound. Donna began trembling and begging "Mistress no please don't make me". Julie waned to taste her and she began oral assault on her. Donna could only drop her head back down and turn it from side to side gasping, "NO, NO please Mistress". Suddenly Donna's body went rigid as she began cumin. Her hips began shuddering and suddenly Julie then attacked Donna's quivering pussy again. Not to be undone, Donna attacked Julie's wet and excited pussy above her.

Now I could see Julie's plan. The way they were positioned, all I had to do was move forward and I would be balls deep in her delicious pussy. Suck momma's cunt My Pet. I have to surprise for you if you do it good enough. This excited Donna and she wanted to make Julie feel as good as she had made her. It wasn't long before Julie squealed, yes My Pet, Momma's going to cum.

With that she humped down on Donna's mouth and flooded her with her juices. Grinding her switching cunt on Donna's tongue until the orgasm passes/ all the while she was still fucking Donna's pussy with her tongue. Julie raised her head and I turned back to Donna "thank you My Pet", but I always wanted both worlds."

That was my cue and I lunged forward burying my cock in Julie's quivering pussy. Donna's eyes widened as she watched my cock spread Julie's pussy and then slid deep within. On impulse Donna raised up from Julie's clit between her lips sucking it as Julie came again. I began slowly swinging from my chains, causing me to drive my cock in and out of Julie's hot pussy.

Donna raised up and caught my balls in her mouth on one stroke and held me there. Gawd damn you two, fuck momma. Julie screamed…..

Julie was getting something she had never had. I was slowly sliding my cock in and out of her steamy pussy while Donna lay beneath her tonguing her excited clit. She could feel an orgasm building and was trying to hold it off. If either one of them could have gotten a hand loose and run a finger over asshole it would have sent her off like a rocket, but they both were bound as she had control.

Suddenly she rolled free of my cock and Donna's tongue. "Holy shit you two, you almost made me go again that was close". Laying to Donna's side she looked back to my hard cock, Donna followed her eyes and couldn't help but lick her lips. "May I Mistress". Smiling Julie looked down at Donna saying, "Yes My Pet, and clean his cock". As Donna raised her head and began trying to get at my cock, Julie looked up into my eyes mouthing, "Don't let her make you cum, I want it".

I groaned because that little whore before me knew how to suck a dick and had gotten it into her mouth. I could feel her talented tongue dancing along my hard shaft and tried to pull back but couldn't. She had me and was doing everything she could to get what she wanted. Julie noticed me trying to get free of her mouth. Reaching over she ran her finger through Donna's spreaded lips. This caused Donna to scream, "Oh gawd Mistress, wait, please let me finish".

Julie didn't want that to happen though and slid a couple fingers into Donna's silky smooth cunt. Donna couldn't help but release my cock and throw her head back screaming, "oh gawd no Mistress not again. I can't". That didn't slow Julie down though only encouraged her to push harder. Sitting up she used her other hand to start circling and caressing Donna's clit.

That was too much for Donna. The g-spot stimulation alone was driving her crazy and now this sent her over the top. Her body lunged upwards as she screamed "OOOOHHHHHHH" and once again cover Julie's hand and the bed with her cum. Each time her body arched, she squirted a long stream across the bed. After what seemed like minutes, which was only really seconds she fell back on the bed exhausted. Sweat was pouring from her body. Her nipples were pointing at the ceiling and I suspected that if Julie got a hold of them she might bring her off again.

Julie leaned down and pressed her own excited body against Donna's. I couldn't hang much longer and cleared my throat. Julie looked up and smiled shit baby I forgot. Hang on and laughed. Slowly moving on the bed until she is standing, she moved to me.

Standing now in front of me and reaching for my wrist cuffs, she leaned forward whispering cuck them baby and rubbed her stiff nipple between my lips. I eagerly took it into my mouth twirling my tongue across it. Julie released one arm and I dropped it around her waist pulling her harder to me. Groaning she slopped her nipple from my mouth and turned to the other wrist, brushing her other nipple to my lips, give us about 30 minutes and then I will come downstairs for you. Releasing the other hand I wrap it around her push her back onto the bed.

Falling we land with me between her outspread legs. I quickly slam my cock deep into her and start fucking her. Screaming No wait not yet, as I held her down and fucked her hard and fast. She began beating on my shoulders screaming NO, NO, wait gawd no, please don't, but I wasn't listening. I wanted one thing and that was to feel her cumin and cumin hard. She groaned oh gawd and I felt her body release. She started bucking beneath me trying to push me away as she begin soaking me.

Smiling I pulled from her body leaving her to squirt across the bed as I held her legs spread. Cum for your Master I growled. Donna was watching wide eyed as Julie couldn't stop. Her hips bucking widely on the bed, twisting and trying to escape my grasp. Releasing her, she fell back onto the bed panting, "Oh gawd, you are killing me". I laughed saying not yet but maybe later and turned to Donna. She was breathing deep and quick. Did you enjoy watching that? "Yes Sir" she answered. I leaned sown brushing her sweat soaked hair from her face and tenderly kiss her lips.

Then I jump off the bed, shaking my arms trying to get the blood back into them. Damn how long was I hanging there? Julie looked at the clock, hmmm almost an hour. You've got to watch that, it could cause serious damage if left too long. Yes Sir, she answered. Walking to her closet I rummage through it and find an old robe. I slip it on and walk out to see the two lovers kissing again. Release her and I will give you 30 minutes, and turned walking out of the room and downstairs.

Once there I pause thinking very nice and went to the kitchen to fix myself something to eat. I glanced at the clock for a reference but I knew she would be here as I instructed. As I finished up my sandwich and my first cup of coffee I hear her walking down the stairs. Click clack, click clack. I turned to the door and waited. Slowing the click clack got closer until she stepped into the door. She had slipped into her long robe and heels. Hmmm I do love a woman who knows how to dress.

She slowly moved to me as I sat back in the chair facing her. She slowly came into my lad and wrapped her arms around my neck. We sat there sharing long sweet kisses that were leaving us both breathless. Where is she I ask? She's upstairs taking a shower. She has to go home and get ready for work tomorrow. I push Julie's robe open and slop my hand inside to hold her big tit. Hmmmm. I do love to play with you. Julie lays her head back moaning oh gawd, do it, pinch them, as she pushed her nipple to my fingers. I reach up and pull lips to mine as I roll her nipple between my fingers pinching it.

Breaking the kiss she calls, I want you. I want you as I've never been allowed to have you. I release her tit and close her robe looking deep into her eyes I know that I can do that but we'll see. Suddenly Donna burst into the room holding her phone the asshole wants to know how I'm going to pay for the wasted night. Julie stands up and shakes her head, fuck how much for the night I ask. Julie looks to me and then Donna. 500 dollars. I push Julie from my lap and walk back upstairs. Getting the money I walked back downstairs.

As I approach the kitchen I over hear them talking.

Why don't you quit? Julie asked. I can't, you know that. He pays for my place and everything I have, Donna answered. Julie was silent and then said let me think about something and I will call you. Ok Mistress Donna said as I walked into the room. Dona looked at me as I held out the money, here for the night. She didn't want to take but really had no choice. Reluctantly reaching out she takes the money and moves in to hug me. I take her into my arms and leaning down I kiss her. He immediately grinds her luscious body into my saying, I owe you Sir. I smile and release her going back and pouring myself another cup of coffee.

She hugs Julie and says "later then Mistress" and she walks out of the room. We hear the door close and Julie turns to me "well seems we are all alone". I sip the hot coffee saying yep appears that way. Want to go watch the video of the night's action I ask. Julie's eyes widen as she asks, what video? I set my coffee down and walk over to her. And walk over to her. I reach up and firmly grasp a handful of hair pulling her head back, really. Her breaths are deep as she realized that she couldn't hide anything from me. So you want this relationship were we trust each other yet you still want to try and play games with me. No sir, I mean, yes sir. Oh gawd sir, as I rip the robe from her body.

Go to the play room and wait for me.

I command. She stands naked in front of me and drops her head. Yes Sir. She slowly turns and walks away. I stand sipping my coffee and then head to the basement. There I find all the recordings set up and cue them up to play, selecting the play room monitor and bed room monitors.

Then I go upstairs and enter the play room. You really want to continue trying my patience. No Sir. I'm sorry Sir. I turn on the monitor and it quickly fills with the scene from earlier in her bedroom. Her eyes wide, how did he know she thought?

So now you will have to be punished and punished severely. Her breath caught in her throat. He's never done this before, she thought. You will several instruments and lay them here, I pointed to a table. Then you will secure yourself there, pointing to the bench in which she had been bound the night before. However this time you will be strapped across it not along it. Understand. Yes Sir.

18

Turning I walked out of the room and into the bathroom. Starting the shower I climbed in and enjoyed the warm waters running down my body. Stepping out, I dry off and slip the robe back on. Then walking down the hall again I enter the play room. Julie is there, secured across the bench. Her ass raised up and exposed. I walk around her checking her blinds. She is secure. Good job. She knows better than to respond but she does so anyway. Yes Sir. I stop in my tracks.

She has always endured whatever I had done with her. I had never heard our safe word until the other night, before and even then she was using it to tease. She was an experienced sub and I still didn't know the depth of her experience. Picking up a paddle I step up behind her and begin paddling her sweet ass until its glowing red. Oh my gawd you fucking freak. You get off on punishing me, don't you, she screamed during the paddling but as my arm was tiring, please Sir stop, oh fuck STOPPPPPP.

I walk back to the wardrobe and find the clips with the weights attached still there. Picking them up I move back around to her. Pulling the stool back around, I sit and reach for one of her nipples. Oh no, please not that. You know my nipples are too sensitive for play. I smile as she tries to look up to see me but can't. Who said we were playing as I pinched and rolled her nipple until it was nice and hard. You son of a bitch, don't. Star, Star.

There it was again that word. I paused as my hand was holding the clip and she was watching it. What's wrong? You call yourself a Dom, but you aren't. A Dom would have never allowed me to tie him.

I opened the clip and attached it to her nipple as she screamed, stop oh gawd, not my nipples. I released the weight it and it dropped stretching her nipple with it.

STAR, STAR, you've got to stop. That's my safe word. As I reached for her other nipple, taking it between my fingers and rolling it before pinching, I know it is and ten I clamped that nipple dropping the weight. You mother fucker, stop it I'm serious, let me up. I stand up and move behind her. She pushes forward enough for the weights to drop to the floor and take some of the strain off her nipples. However I've had to tighten the clips so that they were severely pinching her nipples.

Grasping for breath she continues, you can't do this to me. I told you my safe word. Oh but remember I'm not a real Dom so I don't know what a safe word is. You asshole you know exactly what the fucking safe word is now let me up. I picked up a flogger and went to work on the backs of her thighs. After the first lass, she had raised up squealing holy mother of gawd no causing the weights to pull on her grossly extended nipples. I continue the lashing until the thighs were a nice deep shade of red.

Then walking back around, I drop the flogger in front of her face. Sitting down I grasp a handful of hair and raise her head. So you like playing games. Her eyes are alive with such emotion oh gawd mike you have to stop. I can't take anymore. Please I drop her head and walk over to a candle. Picking it up, I light it and walk back to her. Now waiting as the candle heated up, I tilt it letting the stream of hot was roll down her back.

Her body stiffened immediately as she tried to raise up but she couldn't. The heavy weights tugged at her nipples as she screamed NOOOO, what the fuck. I smile waiting for the wax to build up again and this time tilt it down from her ass down the back of her thigh. Twisting wildly she howls you fucking prick. I was going to fuck you like you've never been fucked today.

Now though I'm going to do to you what I did to that sorry ex-husband of mine. You remember. You watched you son of a bitch. Now let me go.

Smiling I waited for the next pool of wax and then did the other thigh. Holy shit why are you doing this to me.

Stop. STAR, STAR. I set the candle down and once again sat down in front of her. She relaxed her body, letting the weights touch the floor again. Raise up. What. I said raise up. No you asshole I won't, my nipples will be ripped off. I reached down grabbing another hand full of hair and pulled her head up effectively rising he up.

YOU SON OF A BITCH NOOOOOOOOOOOO, and I dropped her head smiling. I know I couldn't leave her that way any longer and reached beneath her unclamping her nipples. She groaned it's about time you fucking dick. Now let me up/ I laughed and said don't run off as I walked out of the room and down to my car. I had something new I was wanting to try and it seemed now was as good a time as any......

As I walk out of the room, I go over into Julie's room and slip on my jeans. Then I go out to my car and grab one of my bags. Bringing it inside I go into the guest room downstairs and find what I'm looking for. Smiling I pick up the box and head back up stairs. There I find Julie wiggling around trying to get free of the horse. I smile gawd what a sight. That sweet ass of hers sticking up just begging for some cock. The wax has dried and coated her body in pale colors. Almost like she had been covered in cum.

Moving back into the room, I sit the box on the table and then walk back over sitting in front of Julie. Did you miss me, baby. She lifted her head growling you son of a bitch, I know you want to fuck me just do it and let me go. HMMMM you have missed me. I reach under her and cup her big tits. She groans, fuck baby, you know how sensitive those are as she tries to get free of my grasp.

HMMMMMMM they seem to have recovered nicely from earlier. She raised her head as much as she could saying oh gawd no, not the clips. No baby not the clips. I've got a new little toy I've been wanting to try with you. Shaking her head, no please don't hurt me anymore. I stand back up and go to the table. I take out the vacuum and two smaller tubes and a larger cup. Then I separate the hoses and lay everything out.

What are you doing? Let me go damn it. I take the two smaller tubes, and sit down in front of her again. I attach a hose to a tube and then to the pump. I place it on my leg and pump the pump. Then I reach for the valve at the base of the tube and release it. I then get up and go to the wardrobe and get a small tube of lube. Sitting back down again I smear a little lube on my fingers as I reach around smearing it around both nipples.

Oh baby yeah that feels better, she groans. I then place a tube over her nipple. What the fuck is that. I then pump the pump and watch as the nipple is pulled into the tube. Oh shit! That feels weird. I then close the valve at the end of the tube and do the other nipple. Now I take two tubes from there and bring them to a y and attach them.

Hey, this kind of feels good she squeals. I smile and move back to the table picking up and cup. Once again I connect a tube walk back to her. I smear some lube around her mound. Yea baby I knew you wanted this pussy. Do it. Fuck me baby and fill me with that cum.

Laughing I then place the cup over her mound and pump it a couple of times, drawing her pussy into the cup. OHHHHH wait baby, what's that? I then seal it off and hook back up to the tubes to her nipples. I then begin pumping, drawing her nipples further and further into the tubes. Holy shit stop now, stop gawd damn it. Her nipples filled about 2/3 of the tube. I'm not some cow you are trying to milk asshole, stop it.

I then pump a few more times drawing her swollen nipples thicker into the tubes. I seal it and connect the pump to her pussy cup. Holy shit you asshole, it feels like someone is trying to suck my tits off. Take them off, please. I then begin pumping the pump drawing her pussy further and further into the cup. Wait oh now. You're pulling me inside fucking out, I continued pumping and watched as her pussy opened and clit jumped into the cup. Stop, stop it hurts, god damn you stop. I then pumped it a couple more times before sealing it off. Now standing back I admired my work.

Both nipples were being pulled deep into the tubes and her swollen pussy filled the other cup. I then walked over and picked up the crop. Walking back to her I asked you feeling good baby. Oh yea baby, I feel good when you let me go I'm going to get even with you. I then walked behind her and began striping her legs. Her wiggling made the tubes shake causing her to moan shit baby stop. Just fuck me and get it over with.

I worked the crop around until I was flicking it against the underside of each tit. Its big flesh turning a nice shade of red as she squealed, release them please. You can spank you all you want but release tem gawd they are throbbing.

I didn't know how long I could leave her hooked up and reluctantly moved to the stool to release her gorgeous swollen nipples. As I turned the valve the base of the first tube, her nipples only shrank back a little.

I the gently screwed the tube from her nipple. It left it swollen and thick. Oh gawd look at me. What have you done, she screamed? I then released the other nipple and it too was swollen and thick. Look how fucking big they are. Shit what have you don't. I then reached out and began rolling them between my fingers. Holy shit, no baby no you're going to make me, no, no, you can't I released them and moved back around behind her.

Reaching down I released the valve on the cup and with a pop it came off her pussy. It too was left swollen and puffy. I set the cup down and leaned over running my tongue over her swollen lips. She nearly jumped off the bench as she screamed NOOOOOOOO. You can't make me you son of a bitch. I won't cum I won't. Standing up, I dropped my jeans and took my cock in my hand. I rubbed it along her swollen pussy and then pushed it in. she groaned. Oh yea, that's what I need. Come on baby, do it.

I bend down and reach around her to find her tits. I grab her swollen nipples and pinch as he screams NOOOOOOOOOOOOOOO. I feel her covering me again. I pull free and watch as jet after jet was squirt cross the room. Smiling I smacked her ass, saying that's a good girl. I then picked up my toys, cleaned them and put them away.

Turning back to her she laid there almost passed out. I walked over and untied her legs. Then I united her arms. I helped her up and carried her out of the play room and into her room. Her bed was still a mess so I laid her on her couch. So she opened her eyes saying gawd that was intense. I picked up a throw and wrapped it over her.

I went into her bathroom and ran her a hot bath. Then came back in, picked her up and took her to her bath. I slowly lowered her into the tub and asked want something to drink? Yea something cold please. I went downstairs and got her something to drink, took it to her and left her to relax. In her room. I stropped the soaked sheets from her bed and the rubber sheet. I took them downstairs to the laundry room and started the wash. Then back upstairs I fix her bed as she steps out of the bathroom.

Wow! Thank you baby. Sure you need to get some rest. I'll send you a text later. I'm going back to my room and get some rest. You can rest here, she smiled. HMMM you know what will happen if I get in that bed with you. She pouted saying, would that be bad? No but I've got something in mind and you can help me out. Her eyes widened and sparkled. Can I? I'll text you later, now get some sleep.

I left and drove back to my room. There I made a few calls. A friend of a friend of mine was getting married next week and y friend wanted to give him a party. Calling all the friends I checked if they could get in town quick enough for tonight. They all said they could. So I set it and told them to be at her address at 9:00.

Next I texted Julie and told her to meet me for dinner at 6. Then I crawled into bed and got some sleep. When I woke up, I showered and got dressed. Arriving at the restaurant I went to the bar and waited. A few minutes before 6 Julie shows up. She's wearing a very nice tight skirt and silky blouse. The way her tits were mobbing beneath it, I could tell she wasn't wearing a bra. Her nipples were barely little nubs beneath her blouse.

I stood and held out my arms as she walked to me. Taking her in them I pulled her close and we kissed. Gawd I could kiss that girl all night. Groaning she pushed me back whispering asshole my tits are sore as shit. Glancing down I groan HMMM they look good. I guess so. They are still swollen and if they weren't sensitive enough before they are doubled now.

Interesting are you hungry. I motioned for the waitress and she showed us to our table. As we sat and enjoyed dinner, she tells me her plan to let Donna move in with her as her sub. She didn't want Donna to have to hook anymore. I nodded saying, sounds like a plan. Smiling her eyes a live again she says then you will have two playmates when you come over.

Nice I say. After the waitress clears the table Julie sits back asking so what can I do for you?

I look up into her eyes saying tonight there are going to 8 guys in your basement to attend a party for one of them. He's getting married in a week. You will entertain them. I then waited as she comprehended what I had said. Can I ask Donna to come help me? I shrugged I didn't think of that but sure if you want. Let me text her and see if she can.

A minute later her phone beeped and it was from Donna. Looking up Julie said, Donna she would love to but doesn't know if her pimp will let her. Well ten tell her to quit, pack her stuff and head to your place, but what about her pimp. I'll take care of that, what's his number? She gives me the number. Now what I want you to do, is go back to your place and get ready. Donna and you are to stay upstairs until I text you to come down. Got it.

She nods her head yes. Ok you head home and let me take care of this other business. I stand up and walk her out to her truck. She turns as she opens the door and I quickly move against her. Holding her tight I kiss her deeply as my hands move over her body. Gawd I would love to do nothing more than to take this woman away to some hide away on the beach, but I couldn't. This was her life and if I wanted to see her, it would be this way.

I call a friend that happens to be on the local police dept. I ask him to meet me at a bar. I also set Donna's pimp to meet me there too. I walk in and see the pimp at the bar. He's a twerp and I walk up to him introducing myself. My friend then walks in and over to me. I introduce him to her pimp. Then I explain that he is not her property any longer and for him not to try and contact her. If he did then I would be back with my fiend to make his little life a bit more complicated. He didn't like but accepted it.

I thanked my friend and asked if he would like to have some fun tonight. Grinning he said, always. We then drove over to Julie's. I parked in the drive and then showed him around. He said he knew Julie but didn't know Donna. I told him that he couldn't tell anyone about either of them. He looked puzzled. I then told him they were going to be tonight's entertainment. His mouth dropped Julie, oh yea and she's sweet. Gawd I know I've seen her around but she's married to some asshole. He's gone.

So tonight I need you to help with security. Sure he agrees. There will be 8 men coming. I will take them to the basement and showed him the route we would take. Walking down the stairs he laughs wow, now this looks interesting. Evidently had been busy. Not only was the pool table cleaned, there was a sex swing hanging in one corner, the couches were arranged so some were facing the swing and the others faced the stripper pole. I would have never guessed he said.

I then turned and we walked back upstairs. Now Julie and Donna are upstairs getting ready, when the guest are here I will text them to come down. Once they come down no one is to enter the basement. Ok, no one enters after the ladies. That's it my friend. So I don't get to see the show. Smiling I pat him on the back saying oh no my friend. You get the best seat in the house, and pointed to the huge monitor showing the basement. So we're set I ask yep I'm good. I went around checking on the drinks and everything looked to be set up. Julie had out done herself.

No I'd see just what the old girl had. Tonight would take her a bit further than we had ever gone. I didn't know if she had ever entertained that many men but we hadn't together. We had a party with a couple of guys but that was it. I turned and walked up stairs knocking on her door. She asked from the other side yes. It's me she cracked the door smiling you'll have to wait like the rest of them. I smiled and held out the little vial of ecstasy. Oh baby I don't know. Up to you.

Taking the vial she leaned out kissing me saying, why not and closed the door. I held the lock turn and smiled as I walked away. As I walked down the hall I noticed the playroom door closed. Checking it, it was locked also. Good I thought. The guys arrived in two long stretches.

Stepping out they were all in suits and looked to be around 30-40 year olds. All looked to be rather well to do. He stepped out and looked around saying Mike, I smiled and walked out hugging him. Glad you could make it. One guy said kind of out of the way though. Yea but it will be worth it, trust me. My friend grinned saying oh my gawd this is going to be sweet. He never lets me down. I turn saying if you will follow me we will get this party started.

We walk through the house as they all commented, nice. Then we walked down to the basement. They all glanced around and settled in. I motioned the bar saying help your selves. Your entertainment will be down shortly. I then cut some music on and turned the TV's on. I then texted Julie. Ready.

Over the music I could hear the click clank, of heels walking towards the basement door. I hear it open and turn. As I hear the click, clack down the stairs. All the men turn looking. Julie and Donna come down dressed in very, very, nice evening gowns. They look like a hundred of bucks. Gentlemen, let me introduce your hostess. And this is Julie. She steps down and smiles to the guys. And this is Donna. She steps down and twist around for the guys. I clap and the guys join in. Now I will leave you in very good hands, and head for the stairs as the guys are introducing themselves to Julie and Donna. Julie turns as I pass and I wink making my way up the stairs.

Finding my friend I say ok no one else down those stair. He laughs saying gotcha boss. Ok I've got some errands to run and I'll be back later. Enjoy the show and walk out of the house....

As the security watched on the camera he didn't really see anything much going on so she figured he'd make himself a drink. Downstairs Julie was wearing long red velvet dress with a slit up the backside to die for, and Donna was wearing a black one, neither girl was wearing a bra nor panties under the dresses, the only other thing they had on was black stilettos 8 inch as always. Julie loved her heel even in boots, about 30 minutes had passed since the girls had taken the ecstasy and it was starting to hit both of them.

They were still talking when one of them stood up and walked over and turned the TV off and turned the stereo up and he said well now let's get this party started dance for us girls. The girls started to dance and Donna went to the stripper pole and started making her body move in ways Julie had never seen before. This was hot even for Julie. So Julie walked over and went behind her grabbing her hips and pressing her hips to hers.

Very turned on by Donna's movements and the ecstasy. Julie leaned forward and whispered in her ear would you like to give them a real show. Donna feeling very horny and wet smiled saying sure. Julie stopped from dancing and turned her around the room got silent except for the music.

Julie then started to take Donna's dress off very slow and sensual the security guard was back watching and called Mike, not knowing if this was acceptable. Mike answered the phone and he explained what was happening, Mike said its fine, but turn the button on the monitor so you can hear them if they say stop, get down there.

The guard said ok and hung up. He turned the button and sat back and watched. Julie had Donna's dress down to her waist and leaned over and started kissing her neck making her tongue, well, seen to the guys. She ran her tongue down Donna's nipple. Donna moaned and leaned back on the pole oh my gawd what are you doing to me? Julie started to suck on Donna's nipple the guys started to moan and say yea there you go take it all off...

Julie slowly lowered Donna's dress more licking as she went down her dress hit the floor and Julie started to lick Donna's very hot wet pussy. She put a finger inside Donna at the same time this caused Donna to moan very loud.

Julie looked up at her and said follow me she lead Donna to the pool table she had placed a plastic sheet on it already. Donna climbed up on the table, Julie looked at the guys and said, HMMMM will someone help my up please. Two of the guys jumped up saying hell yea. Once she was on the tale Donna helped Julie out of her dress and before anyone realized Julie said now my pet eat me all the guys stood up and gathered around the table as Julie laid back as she ordered Donna to eat her in front of all of them.

Julie reached up and grabbed something she had hid under the corner of the sheet... it was a vibrating wand. Julie smiled when Donna seen whet she had. Julie spoke up and said can I get one you to hold this on her clit and don't let her take it off. This very well built black man I will and took it from Julie. Both girls were so hot right now a bomb could go off and they wouldn't have cared they needed a release. All the guys by now had a hard on you could see it bulging out of their pants.

Donna began to lick very slowly up and down Julie's still swollen pussy from earlier. Julie moaned with excitement, oh yes my! My Pet, make mamma cum, come on. Donna put two fingers inside her pussy and began to pump them in and out going faster and faster as she started to run her tongue faster and faster. The black man was so amazed he had forgotten he had the wand in his hand, he kink of shook his head and turned it on he placed it on Donna's clit she screamed NOOO, you're going to make me cum...

Julie spoke up and said that's the idea My Pet. I want you to cum. the closer Donna came to cumin the faster she ran her tongue on Julie's clit. Julie started to moan, YES, YES, YES, and started to squirt all over Donna's face. Donna started to suck on her pussy to get every drop she was releasing as she was, Donna grabbed Julie's hips and said shit, oh gawd yes. I'm cumin the man started moving back and forth. Donna was losing control fast she kept cumin and still kept sucking and fingering Julie. Julie was ready to cum again and she didn't want to yet. Julie pushed her head back and she said not yet. She told the man to stop for a minute. Julie looked and two of the guys had their jackets off and had their cocks in their hand trying to get some relief, the girls had all of them turned on.

Julie was very turned on as well was Donna. Julie knew she could take the guys to the limit, but she realized she really didn't want to. She wanted Mike even just as a friend she had decided long ago she would settle for that and she knew she could be happy with that. About then Donna started in her old habits and started playing with the guys. Julie grabbed her hair and said oh no My Pet you're mine and you don't play unless told. I haven't finished with you yet come with me.

Julie went to the swing and sat in it. It was just high enough that Donna could kneel in front of her and still reach her. Donna knelt in front of her and started to lick Julie's clit. Julie started moaning one of the guys went behind the swing and reached down and started to play with her tits. Oh gawd, Julie said stop or you will make me cum. Just about then he started to pinch her nipple. Julie moaned oh yes please make me cum.

Donna started to finger her and licking faster. Julie leaned back in the swing as her head went back and realized it was Mike, he had snuck back in and she hadn't noticed. Julie smiled at him and said gawd I've missed you. Julie was about to cum and looked deep in his eyes and said fuck me please I need you inside me.

Mike came around and told Donna to amuse herself for a little and pointed to the guys. When he was in front of Julie still in the swing he pulled his hard cock out of his pants and slowly started to fuck Julie. Pushing her back and forth in the swing, making it go deeper and deeper inside her. Julie moaned Mike reached down with one hand and started to play with her clit, which that was all it took. Julie exploded with delight omg. She had never felt such a release before without toys and this man was able to make her so cum so hard...

Donna was enjoying herself she had made her way on to the pool table and was laying across it. She was sucking one man's cock while another was fuckign her and another held a vibrating wand on her clit she was so excited her body was jerking. Julie and Mike were just watching. Julie wrapped her arms around Mike and said I know you not my Dom, however, we can be friends and maybe more in time. Donna was getting louder and louder, now she came so hard she squirted all over the table.

Julie know she was just dreaming about being with mike and that was ok. She knew there wasn't a future there, but she really did enjoy being with him at times and talking with him. She had never been able to open up with someone before she was content with friends though just about then Mike said Hmmmm, let's get things rolling her and told Donna to get back to her Mistress...

The guys were all in a high state of excitement. Several had already stripped and were either fucking Donna or trying to make her cum. The rubber sheet was soaked beneath her where she had already cum a couple of times. Donna reluctantly crawls off the pool table. Several guys help her down and in the process take advantage to squeeze her nice tits and ass. She giggles and wiggles walking away to Julie.

Julie stands with her arms out as Donna walks in to them and they hug. Ok ladies, time for some refreshments I say. They both move over to the bar area as a couple of guys crowd around them. The others are sitting around the couches smoking cigars and watching the shows. Most have taken their coats off and loosened their ties. Sever of these guys are the most powerful of the group. You can tell by their reserved attitudes. I really don't know them except for my friend. He ask could Julie get them something to drink. Looking at him haying they wouldn't prefer Donna. No, they Requested Julie.

I nod to Julie as she moves around to me. Go check on these guys. They asked for you personally. Smiling she moves over to the couches introducing herself again I watch but had to turn away because I know she's there to entertain and it still kind of bothers me. I wasn't yet ready to accept my feeling for her and I wasn't going to appear weak to her. Moving over to the pool table, I slide the sheet off and rack up the balls. One of the guys comes over and we begin a game. Glancing over to the group on the couches, I seem them waiting for Julies' return...

As the game progresses, the party hits rhythm. Julie and Donna are moving through the crowd serving the guys and getting felt up along the way. For the most part pretty tame. I shoot a couple games and then step away. I hear a few squeals as Julie and Donna are pulled on guys laps and squeezed, but nothing the girls didn't seem to be able to handle.

So, I make my way to the stairs to go up and check on my buddy at the door. As I do though I notice one of the guys sitting on the sofa group is watching me pretty intensely. I shrug it off and walk on up the stairs. Upstairs, I ask how it's going, quite he answers then looking at the big monitor says, looks like it was getting pretty hot down there.

Laughing I say yea it was going to get out of hand if I didn't slow things down. He laughed groaning. Damn Julie is hot. I've seen her around town and she's always seemed to, I don't know, untouchable. Well behind closed doors, we tend to be a bit different than what we portray in public. I hope you don't mind but damn watching you fuck her. WOW! I laugh again saying yea WOW!

I step outside for a few minutes getting some fresh air. The night is clear and mild. The sky is lit up with stars. My mind drifted back to my dream of the beach. Picturing myself sitting back enjoying he calm. My buddy opened the door saying, you might want to come look at this. I turn and walk back inside. Looking at the monitor, I see the black guy who was watching me so intently, pumping his, obviously, fucking one of the girls in the swing. Two of the other suits were standing beside him probably playing with her tits.

Looking about the room to figure who they had cornered, I see Donna at the bar and three guys keeping her busy. So they must have Julie in the swing. I watch a bit more and now see Julie's legs wrap around his ass, pulling her harder to him mu cock stiffens watching her heels kicking with each thrust.

20

Y ou don't mind them fucking her. Well it's not that I don't mind, it's just not mine to mind. Get the difference. Nodding he groans damn don't know if he's getting the best of it or if she is.

We watch as the guy pulls out shooting his load across her stomach and her tits. One of the squeezing her tits, releases her, opens his pants and moves between her spread legs. Then stepping closer, slips into her red hot pussy. Now he legs raise up until they are over his shoulders as he begins fucking her. Glancing across the room I see that now the guys have Donna dancing on the bar.

I figured that Julie would hold back as long as I was there, so I knew I had to leave the room. Plus the ecstasy was now at full strength and she wouldn't be able to stop herself. So I tell my friend well I'm going back downstairs. As I made my way down the stairs I could hear Julie growling, come on asshole, you call that a dick, fuck me spurring her partner on. As I came around the corner I could see Julie's legs kicking the ass of the man between them.

Almost like she was trying to ride him like a horse. Her black partner had stepped away and was now standing at the bar watching Donna shake her tits. Two other black guys had moved over working on Julie's big tits as the little guy pounder away at her.

With a loud groan he tries to pull free but soaks Julie's pussy with his cum as it covers her swollen mound. HMMMMMM. Gawd baby you save that up for a while didn't you. Smiling shyly he pulled his pants up and moved back away almost embarrassed for letting his emotions run away with him. Later I would find out he was a minister at the groom's church. The two black guys now standing with Julie suspended between them squeezed her big tits and pinched her nipples causing her to continue, oh fuck yea, and look at those big black hands squeezing my poor white tits.

One reached up and loosened a strap which allowed Julie to lean back more, almost vertical.

Looking at her two new partners Julie moans. I hope one of you has at least a dick big enough to let me cum. The two men smile looking down at their hot white prize. Pulling upwards on her stiff rubbery nipples one says, you ever bad a black cock before. Not till just a minute ago. Ever had two black cocks before. Her eyes widen as one steps between her, spread her logs and the other moves around to the top of her head.

Julie raises her head and watches as the guy between her legs slowly begins to open his slacks. As he does, her eyes watch until his fat black dick droops into view. Holy shit, as she kicks her heels rubbing her cum soaked little pussy against it. Taking it in his hands, he rubs the fat purple head through the juices saying this will come in handy, as he pushes the head between her lips. The swing rocks back pushing her head against the guy standing behind her. Fuck your thick. Go slow you black son of a bitch. He holds still as she lays her head back with a deep groan.

The man standing behind her then begins opening his slacks. Her eyes, widen as he grabs the straps suspending her arms. The one starting to bury his long thick black cock in her grabs the one holding her hips. Raising his cock he slaps it across her face saying, come on baby open wide for daddy. Julie can't stop herself as her tongue slips out and across the huge plum head. Then slowly wrapping her lips around it she starts sucking it like a baby sucks its thumb. Oh yea momma suck it. He growls.

Looking up at his partner, he signals and then they begin. The one wanting to fuck her pulls against the strap, pulling her further onto his horse cock. The one she is sucking releases his grip and steps a little closer. Now as the one fucking her releases and the one she's sucking pulls. Since he stepped closer she is forced to take more of his cock into her mouth.

Both men continue stepping closer until the one fucking here has his cock buried to his big black balls and the one she is sucking, is sliding down her throat with her nose brushing his hanging balls. Each swing back onto her partner's cock would leave her gasping but she wouldn't try to hold them back. She wanted it and wanted everything. On one swing she slipped the cock from her mouth screaming oh gawd you're making me cum, and squirted all over the man between her legs.

The crowd cheered as she continued holy fuck, you two are splitting e into give me those big black dicks, and that's just what they did. They continued fucking her for about 15 minutes until they both yelled. Let's fill her up and let loose their seed into her.one filling her dropping pussy and the other pumping his down her throat.

Watching you could see her throat constricting around the huge cock. As both guys stepped back and pulled their slacks up the one between her legs groans she soaked my slacks. His partner saying holy shit that white bitch can fuck. Then turning to Julie they helped her from the swing. As she stood up cum was running down her thighs and down her chin across her big swollen tits. I need a drink she moaned as she made her way to the couch.

As she sat down, two more guys moved to each side of her one handed her a drink while the other introduced them to her. Julie took the drink and sipped it as they continued talking.

Donna in the mean, time stopped dancing on the bar. I had moved behind it and was tending bar as she had been pulled from atop it onto a guy's lap as he sat at the bar. She was slowly grinding against him as she sucked and chewed on her sweet big stiff nipples. Leaning back against the bar, I bring a bottle of tequila up and hold it over her mouth.

Open wide she leans back looking at me and then the bottle and opens her mouth. I pour a generous amount of tequila into her mouth. Until she turns away. Leaving me poring the liquor down her chest. The guy sucking her tits goes to licking and sucking the liquor from her. Looking back at him she reaches down and opens his slacks.

Then raising up she pulls his stiff cock free. Then she slowly lowers back down taking him fully into her horny pussy. Oh gawd fuck me she whispers as she begins bouncing on his lap. He tries to hold the bar as she begins getting wilder and wilder on his cock. Her tits bouncing in his face as she rides him. He tries to hold back but cant and soon is whining shit, shit I'm going to cum. She smiles saying do it, and rides him until there is nothing left for her to ride. Slowly pulling from his lap, she leaves a trail of cum across his thighs and hers.

My friend then stand saying ok its time the groom got his dance. He then walks to the side of the room where the pole stood. He takes a chair with him and sets it down. I look at Donna and then at Julie. Ok guys let's give the ladies a chance to freshen up for the grooms dance. I then take Donna's hand and reach out for Julie's. She slowly gets to her feet and I lead them back upstairs.

As I reach the top of the stairs, my buddy steps up need me to help. Yea help get them upstairs and back down here in 30 minutes. I look at Julie and Donna you ok. Julie's eyes are glazed over yea I'm fine, just give me a few minutes. Take a quick shower and dress up for your lap dances. Donna giggles. HMMMMM. He's got a nice big cock. I felt it when I was at the bar. Julie's eyes widened holy shit did you see those two that fucked me. I thought they were going to split me into. Both started laughing as he helped them upstairs. I turned and went back down stairs......

Both girls were very wore out. They went into the bedroom and both sat on the edge of the bed. Julie looked in the mirror across from her and said wow. I'm a mess and then looked at Donna and said well I don't feel so bad so are you and let out a little chuckle.... Julie stood up and said we need to shower there expecting us back in 30 minutes Donna said ok but can we grab something to snack on Julie said yes I'll call down stairs.

She picked up the phone knowing Mike said would answer and asked if he would make a sandwich and cut it in half please. Mike said sure take a shower it will be in the room waiting when you girls got in the shower knowing it wasn't going to be just a quick shower. Mike started to the kitchen. The girls got in the shower.

Donna started to rub the soap on Julie's breast she moaned a little saying gawd that feels so good even though they are sore. Donna smiled and worked her way down to Julie's still swollen pussy. Julie backed up to the wall and opened her legs a little more Donna scrubbed her clean down there and then knelt in front saying may I mistress?

Julie said yes but we can't be long. Donna knew it wouldn't take long Julie was still so excited over the evenings events. Donna licked her clit a couple of times and then shoved two fingers inside her. Julie moaned. Donna went faster and harder inside her and Julie grabbed her head pushing her face deep into her pussy saying eat me gawd damn it make me cum harder. Donna did as she was told, Julie soon came hard. Donna stood up in front of her and said I think I will like living with you Mistress. Julie smiled and said yes I think I will enjoy it also.

The girls finished showering and dried off and came out of the bathroom to find a very nice sandwich and two glasses of wine. Julie sat down and started to eat so did Donna. Julie glanced at the clock and said shit we only have fifteen minutes we need to hurry and figure out what figure out what we are wearing... Donna smiled and said well it seems your Mike already thought of that Julie said what.

Donna pointed to the couch in the room a bright red velvet Victorian couch very old and on it was some of Donna's stripper outfits. Both with a note. One said Julie, I thought you would look great in this and the other one saying Donna I hope you like my choice.

Julie started to look at her pile wow he thought of everything a pair of black stilettes with pink lining in them a pair of fish net stocking that were crotch less a garter belt black lace with pink bows and a leather skirt that had Velcro on the sides for easy removal, and a black fish net shirt and a black bra with under wires and a pair of dress nipple clips with a gold chain connecting them so they could be seen through the shirt and a black color that the chain of the clips went through. WOW! HMMMMMM! This is going to be fun she said. What did he pick out for you Donna?

A pair of red stilettes and something that looked like a short, short jumper outfit and a black bra with nipple clips and a g string. Donna said ok let's see what this looks like. Donna started to get dressed as did Julie. When Donna was done she actually looked cute they were shorts and top together the shorts were very short and again the outfit Velcro's up the side it was shinny almost like a plastic on the back in faded lettering said FBI. There was a badge that read FBI, female body inspector, Donna chuckled. Oh gawd the guys are going to love this.

Julie came back in the room WOW! You look hot with her she also had a whip. Julie said well I don't know if the guys will like this or run... I'm sore so I'm hoping for run. I just want Mike to hold me I don't know how much more I can do of this I'm only doing it because he told me to and in hopes he will get jealous. Donna being Donna said whatever I'm having fun. I hope this night never ends, and with that the girls headed down the stairs to the main floor.

I went back downstairs after getting Julie and Donna upstairs. I was a little concerned for them but they seemed to be aware of what had been going on. Hopefully they would take a quick shower as I had suggested. Downstairs to the guys had all put all their cocks away and pulled their pants up. When I reached the bottom of the stairs they turned to me and I heard a soft groan. I know they wanted to get back at the girls but I also knew it would be hard the girls letting the guys have their way. I thought too much of Julie and Donna to let that happen.

Oh I had been part of parties where we had let the guys have the girls and didn't hold back. By the end of the night the girls were left on their backs with cum running out of every hole.

Although very erotic they were put through hell. So I was trying to let the girls catch their breaths and hopefully keep the guys entertained. I walked over to the bar and poured myself a drink.

The first black guy that had fucked Julie came over to the bar asking, excuse me but so they book these parties regularly. I looked up saying NO, it's a onetime party for them. Then I lied their husbands are out of town and will be back early tomorrow morning. He groaned shit she is hot. I raise my glass saying that she is. He moves away from the bar and back to the little group.

Then I move over and start sliding the couch around so that all seats were facing the show area. We had the groom's chair set up and using a couple of the overhead lights, I turn them to the spotlight area. Stepping back I look at the stage and it looks pretty good. As I'm standing there the black guy comes back up asking, after the dance are the ladies going to hang around any longer. I knew what he was asking, was I going to get to fuck Julie again, and held my temper back.

Probably will but that will be up to them. He smiled and laughed saying well then we'll just have to make worth their while, and walked back to his group. A cheer went up as he evidently told them that they would have another crack with Julie.

My phone beeped and I read a message from Julie asking for something to eat. I text her back to get in the shower and I would get them something. Walking up the stairs, I ask my buddy if he would fix the girls a sandwich or something and take it to their room. Smiling he said sure. I then turned and went back downstairs.

I knew I was going to have to get out there before the grooms dance was done. If I didn't there might be trouble and I didn't want that for my friend. I looked around and got his attention and motioned towards the pool table. I walked over and he came over after a minute. What's up? I just wanted to talk to you about that little group over there. Hey man I'm sorry I know he can be a real ass but he's the groom's father in law. That surprised me, he's marrying a black girl. Shaking his head Yep.

Shrugged well nothing wrong with that it's just I never would have pictured it. I know it took us by surprise too and her dad isn't very impressed with him. I looked back over at the man as he smoked his cigar and boasted of this and that to the group. Just watch him for me ok. He's a bit aggressive and I don't want any trouble or the girls getting hurt. Oh shit I agree, man. That Donna is something, I laughed saying you horny piece of shit, get away from me and walked back over to the bar.

Checking the clock I saw I had 10 minutes before the girls were due to be back. So I grabbed some snacks and a couple of beers and headed upstairs to my buddy. I sat down with handing him the food and a beer. I opened mine saying, I am having doubts about this. He looks at me, what's going on. I might have some trouble downstairs with a group of guys. Well just beep me and we'll toss their asses out. I smile saying thanks, I was hoping I could count on you.

21

Then we heard the click clack of heels coming down the stairs. I turned to and almost fell out of my chair. Holy shit Julie looked good and Donna, wow. My buddy punched me in the ribs saying, looking good huh. I shook my head gawd yes she looks great. Julie walked straight to me, pressing her body to mine and looking into my eyes. Hey Mister having a good time. I smile fuck you look good. Stepping back so I could see everything she grins, you have good taste.

Well the boys are getting restless down there, you ready. Julie looks to Donna who smiles nodding let's do it. As we walk to the door I tell them that I had told the party that their husbands would be back early in tomorrow. They nod and Julie says good cause I don't want this to last all night. I've got someone I'm waiting to some time with. She reaches out and wraps herself in my arms and we share a long hot kiss leaving us both breathless. Damn girl. I groans I reach for the door knob you don't have to open it you know. We could go back upstairs and put this show on for you.

I turn and look into her eyes. She can feel my jealously building and she knows that she will have to be careful or it would blow up. I look over to Donna and I can see she doesn't care one way or the other. I made a commitment to my friend I mumble. Well then once we go up to dance for the groom, you better leave. I look into her eyes as she looks down. I know and I guess I will. Julie moves away from me and takes Donna's hand. You ready baby girl, Hell Yea Mistress. Julie then slaps Donna's ass with her whip saying lets go get some and opens the door.

THE RELEASE

The basement goes silent as they hear the door open. The click clack of the heels coming down. They all know whose coming but weren't expecting what was coming. As Julie and Donna entered the room he guys all began cheering and making loud remarks. Oh baby look at those bit tits. Gawd those legs are on for fucking ever. Come here baby, I'll pinch those big nipples for you and many more. I walk down behind them and look over to my friend. He grabs up the groom and takes him to the chair.

Julie and Donna reach the stage area and adjust the groom so he is facing the couches. Then Julie looks to me saying cut the CD labeled dance in. I go over and find it and place it on. I then dim the room lights the stage area lit. The music comes on and Julie asks turn it up. I turn it up louder and she nods. Then looking into my eyes, she nods he head towards the door. I know what she's telling me and I grimace as I walk up the stairs and out of the basement. As I reach the top of the stairs, I hear the group cheer and want to turn around to see what's going on but I don't.

Stepping through the door, my buddy ask you aren't going to watch the show. No but I need you to if it get out of hand beep me. Where are you going? I'm going out to get some fresh air. My old lungs can't talk all that smoke. He nods and turns back to the monitor. I turn and walk out the door. I wanted to so take Julie up on her offer of going back upstairs with her and letting them put their show on for me. Gawd I wish I would have. Now I would have to just let the night finish.

The drugs were still very potent in their systems so, they should be ok. I was still worried about the father in law though. Maybe I was just jealous and that concerned me. I had never been this way before. I walk around the house and up the stairs to the upper deck. I walk around to the hot tub and smile. There laying on the floor was the top to that tiny bikini she had worn the night before. Sitting down I look back out into the stars, what's become of me.

Downstairs the party had begun. Julie and Donna had moved so that each were straddling one of the groom's legs facing him with their backs to the group. Julie looked into his shy excited eyes. Hi baby, we are going to have some fun. Now you are not to touch us until I tell you too. Then leaning forward pressing her big tits into the side of his chest she whispers in the ear, just relax and you will have a great time to remember, and kissed his ear. His face turned a deep shade of red as she sat back throwing her shoulders back. He didn't know whether to look at Julie's big tits or Donna's.

Donna then mirrored Julie's moves. Julie reached up and squeezed her big tits arching her back sliding her crotch against his leg. Reaching up she took his hand and brought it around to squeeze her ass as kept talking low to him. The other guys couldn't hear her but, he could. HMMMM. Our nipple are burning baby. Momma needs you to release them for us. Will you do that baby, his eyes were bouncing back and forth between the sweet set of tits before him. They would have crawled across broken glass at this point to get at either one of them.

Donna purred, oh baby, you will have to kiss each nipple and make it feel better as you release them. Both women were grinding their pussies across his leg to the rhythm of the music. The group was quick, trying to hear what was being said and in awe of the show before them. Each wanted to be the young groom. The big father in law was rubbing his stiff cock planning wishing it was his Julie was grinding on.

Both girls leaned forward kissing his ear and Julie whispered don't go anywhere, we'll be right back. Then they both stood up and turned to the group. The guys all eyed the delicious baby dolls in front of them. Julie in her fishnet shirt and mini skirt and Donna in her latex jump suit. There wasn't a soft cock in the group. Even the minister couldn't help but get a chubby.

Both women were moving to the music. Walking across the make shift stage letting the guys get a good look at them. If they reached for Julie, she would flick the whip at them sending them back to their seats. Donna was so lucky she kept them at bay. Julie made her way back behind Donna and then while looking over her shoulder, she reached around letting her hands cup Donna's nice tits, squeezing them. Donna groaned and laid her head back on Julie's shoulder as her fingers reached up and slowly pulled the zipper down on the jump suit. Slowly Donna's cleavage came into view and then as the zipper reached her belly button, Julie released it and grabbed both sides opening the jump suit causing Donna's tits to jump out into view. The room erupted in cheers.

Julie released Donna and she strutted across the stage. Letting the guys get a nice look at her bouncing tits. Her nipples clipped and aching as her heavy tits shook. Then turning around she showed the guys the badge on the back of the suit and winked at them. Now moving back to Julie she struck a pose in front of her. Then making a little production she patted down Julie's shoulders and made her way around behind Julie. Then placing a leg between Julie's she makes her spread them. The guys are loving it as they all cheer.

Donna then begins patting down Julie. Running her hands down, she sides and down her legs, then slowly back up the inside of Julie's legs. Holding Julie's hip she takes her whip and turns it, pushing from behind Julie and rubbing the stiff black leather handle through her spread legs. As it emerges from between Julie's legs it looks like a big cock jutting out. Donna peeks around Julie's hips, eyes wide and winks at the group as she strokes the black cock causing a round of loud cheers and groans. Dropping the whip her hands now move up and over Julie's big tits. Cupping them and Squeezing causing Julie to groan, shit baby, do it.

Donna slips her fingers between the buttons of Julie's shirt and pulls slightly. Then once again looks to the group with wide questioning eyes. Almost at once they cheer, RIP IT. With a determined look on her face Donna then rips the fishnet shirt open causing Julie's big tits to jump into view. Her shelf bra held them up high and the chain between the two clips shined running up to the collar around Julie's neck. Julie made an attempt to reach up and cover them but Donna quickly ripped the shirt down her arms leaving her in her bra and mini skirt. The group is going absolutely nuts cheering and clapping.

The girls then turn their attention back to the young groom. He was still sitting as Julie had directed and it tickled her and she smiled, oh baby look at you. Be gentle because they are aching badly right now and we need to get these clips off. He can only nod his head as he looks as the 4 big tits in front of him. Their nipples red and very stiff.

Ok baby you can start. He raises a shaking hand and Donna giggles and leans forward feeding him her stiff nipple. He quickly wraps his warm lips around it and just as Julie had instructed, he tenderly caresses it with his tongue. Donna sits back smiling, oh Mistress he did that very well. Julie was caught up in the show now. She was tugging the chain between her nipples. He then reached up and released Donna's other nipple. Once again she leaned forward, feeding him the tit. Reluctantly she pulls away and then stands turning to the group and begins dancing across the stage area.

In the meantime, the groom looked from Julie's big stiff nipples up into her eyes and back to her nipples. Please baby, momma needs you to help her. His hand reaches up and this time he squeezes Julie's big tits causing her eyes to widen, oh you're being naughty, as he released it and opened the clamp. As the blood returned to her nipple Julie gasped and leaned forward feeding it to him, tender baby mammy needs you.

He quickly took it and caressed it with his soft warm tongue. Slowly sitting back up she smiles, that's my baby, oh I am going to take good care of you. He then reaches up squeezing Julie's other tit, causing her nipple to throb, oh you naughty little shit. As he released the clamp and she leaned forward. This time she reached around his head and pulled him to her aching nipple. Do it for momma baby. He did just as she asked and soothed her aching nipple.

Pushing back she smiled don't go anywhere, and stood turning to the group. They all groaned seeing the clips now hanging between her heaving tits. Her nipples still hard as glass. Spreading her legs and putting her hands on her hips she throws her shoulders back. Letting them enjoy themselves. His father in law was in a state of very high arousal. He wanted to go up and slap the shit out of the groom and take Julie back.

The rest of them could have Donna he wanted Julie and it was pissing him off that his son in law was getting to enjoy her. Both girls danced around the stage a few minutes. Julie knew she had to let the young groom calm down or he would end the show too quickly. Sitting on his leg she could feel his long hard cock pressing against her thigh. There was already a nice big wet spot at the tip. She was impressed.

Evidently Donna hadn't been wrong he was hung. Slowly turning back to the young groom, Julie moved to him. Pushing his legs together, she straddled him and leaned forward rubbing her hard nipples across his face and whispering to him, no baby momma needs you to do something else for her. My skirt is held together with Velcro. If you grab it, it will rip apart. Same for Donna's suit. We are going to move on each side of you. First I want you to reach around and rid Donna's from her. Then I want you to reach around and rip momma's, from her. Will you do that for momma, baby. Her nipples were rubbing across his lips as he answered yes Ma'am. Julie smiled saying bite it for momma, baby bite it.

Looking up into her excited eyes he took the nipple between his teeth and bit down. She threw her head back screaming, oh gawd you naughty, naughty boy and jumped from his grasp with a wink.

She then nodded to Donna they took their positons beside the groom. Julie then said well we've enjoyed putting this little show on for you all but before she could finish he made an attempt to over herself as she pranced around the stage. Oh gawd you naughty, naughty boy. Julie stood looking shocked at what he had done when he reached around and ripped her skirt free. Leaving her standing in her shelf bra, garter and fishnets. The group went nuts. Julie dropped her hands to between her legs you naughty boy, you want these men to see momma naked.

Donna then moves back to the young groom. You doing ok baby, she whispers. He doesn't know where to look but he can't help but look at the two big tits in his face now. Baby, Mistress is going to come over here and pull your pants off you. Then she is going to suck that big dick of yours ok. He looked into her lust filled eyes please.

She leaned down and kissed him quickly, oh baby we are going to take good care of you and stepped away.

Julie then turned and marched to the young groom. Well if momma is naked then you need to be too. She then pulled him to his feet and squatted in front of him. She then unbuckled his belt, popped open the button and pulled the zipper down. Then looking up into her eyes she winks and pulls his pants and underwear down with one long stroke. His big hard cock snaps up almost hitting Julie in the face causing her to push back slightly and looking up into his eyes, holy shit baby, and momma is going to love this and licks her red lips. She then pushes him back and he sits down.

Slowly moving forward Julie positions herself between his spread legs. Donna moves around behind him and pulls his head back between her big tits as Julie takes his cock into her hands stroking him. Turning to the group she purrs, HMMMMM, the bride is a lucky girl, and then turning back to him, engulf his cock down her throat. The group lets out a collective groan as they can't believe she could take that whole thing sown her throat. His whole body goes rigid as his hips raise up off the chair.

Donna reaches around and pinches the shit out of his ear love causing his eyes to flash open, we don't want you ending the show before I get some of that. She knew he would lose it and fill Julie's mouth if she didn't distract him. Now running her hands down she pinches the shit out of his nipples as he reaches out to grab Julie's head. NO, NO, baby not allowed, Donna whispers. He drops his head looking up Donna can see that once again he is losing it. She quickly pinches his ear lobes as she presses her big tits to his face.

Julie reluctantly releases the young groom's big cock. Gawd there is nothing she liked better than sucking a nice big hard dick and this one was perfect. She wanted it but she knew it wasn't time. Slowly raising up, she slipped it between her tits and stroked it looking into his eyes. HMMMMM. Momma likes your big dick. And winks at him. Now I'm going to stand up and pull you up with me. Donna is going to move the chair and take your shirt off. I then want you to lay down for momma, ok.

Julie then stands pulling him to his feet also. She then turns facing the group and backs up against the young groom. Reaching down she takes his hands and brings them up to squeeze her heaving tits. As she does Donna peels his shirt off him.

Turning back Julie almost stops. Holy shit he if fucking gorgeous she thinks. Now naked as the day he was born he starts to get a little embarrassed. Donna reaches around grabbing his hanging cock whispering oh baby, we are going to make a mess all over you, and she strokes him. He tries to turn his head to see her as Julie steps forward looking into his eyes she says loudly can we enjoy this one last time before you give it to her. His eyes widen and glances toward his father in law as he moans. Holy shit.

Julie smiles as they help him lay down and get comfortable. They ask for a pillow from the group and one is tossed onto the stage. The men have moved forward and now so they will be able to see the show. Donna quickly moves around and straddles his hips, reach up and pull my panties off she whispers. Once again with shaking hands he reaches up toughing this beautiful woman and slides her panties down her long legs. She smiles winking at him as she takes them and twirls them out into the group.

She then reaches down, taking his cock in her hand and slowly lowers herself on it. Once it was about 2/3s in she stops oh gawd that thing is stretching me open, and slowly up only to begin sliding back down. His cock is now covered with her shiny coating as she finally takes it deep into her. HMMMM, baby you feel good. He is watching her and wasn't paying attention to Julie as she moved around and straddled his head. Looking down momma needs attention to baby, and slowly starts squatting over the young grooms face.

Instinctively his tongue shot out and slipped between Julie's swollen wet lips. She then starts grinding her hips on his tongue as she purrs, oh yea, fuck momma with that tongue. Soon the threesome is in a groove. Donna slowly fucking up and down his big cock, while Julie fucked his tongue. Julie reaches out and pulls Donna's face to hers and they share a long hot kiss as the group once again goes nuts for the show. Now both women were pulling on each other's, nipples as they gazed into each other's lust filled eyes.

Suddenly Donna squeals and raising up unleashes a stream of juice across his body as her orgasm rushes over her. Julie raises up as the groom looks down watching Donna cum on him. Smiling she leans forward kissing him, thanks baby, your brides is as lucky girl, and she stands up. Julie then moves around to straddle his hip and looking into his eyes saying loudly so no I guess you want momma to take care of this big hard dick.

With that she squats over his cock grabbing it and using it like a dildo rubbing her pussy and clit. Oh baby momma wants to cum. Do you want momma to cum? She then drops down taking as much of his cock into her excited cunt.

Oh shit baby, you are big. Then pulls up and drops back down until she has him deep inside. She then begins fucking him hard come on baby give it to momma. Make her cum baby. Reaching over she takes his hands pinch momma's tits and she will cum for you. He quickly closes his fingers around each hard nipple and pinches down.

Julie ad been close for the last 10 minutes and this did it for her. Let me up, let me up baby she purred as she raised up showing the group as she came all over the young grooms cock. Her juices covering his body as he watched her squirting. Then looking up into his eyes come on baby you can puck momma now, and she rolled over spreading her legs wide.

He quickly followed her moving between her outstretched legs and burying his cock in her quivering cunt. He was too excited to last long and soon he was pounding away at Julie's pussy. Her legs were kicking in the air as he fucked her. Oh baby fuck momma. Gawd that big dick feels so good.

Come on now give it to momma. Her arms wrapped around his shoulders trying to hold on as he drilled her into the floor. Suddenly with a jerk she stiffened and she could feel him swelling inside her, oh baby, momma can feel it and then he filled her hot pussy with his cum. The two continued fucking until she slipped from her soaked cum filled cunt. She held him tight whispering, HMMMMM. That was nice, thank you baby. He looked into her beautiful eyes and almost said I love you but caught himself. Smiling shyly now he rolled off her and the room erupted in cheers and clapping.

Donna helped him, handed him his clothes and gave him a big before pointing to the bathroom so he could get cleaned up. Then turning to Julie she saw her laying there, her legs still spread wide and cum beginning to run from her swollen abused pussy. She reached out and helped Julie to her feet and then the two bowed to the group. Both still naked walked through the group to the bar asking for a drink. One of the guys served them while the others thanked them for such an erotic show.

He couldn't take any more. The father in law stood up and walked to the bar. He then took Julie's arm and led her back to the couch area he had been sitting at. Then sitting down with her, him and two friends started talking to her.

3 other guys took Donna over to the other side of the couch and began talking with her. It all seemed innocent enough at first. The guys were respectful and they all enjoyed their drinks......

But what the girls didn't realize is that the bride's father had cooked up a gang bang whether the girls wanted to participate or not he wasn't going to give them a choice. Everyone was laughing and joking around and then the next thing you know the big black guy looked over to the guys that were with Donna and nodded his head then two from each group grabbed the girls and cuffed them down. Both girls started to scream, the groom was yelling for them to stop but they didn't listen. Mike's buddy saw what was happening and started to ring Mike.

Mike answered he said get back here now the girls are in big trouble. Mike felt his heart go into his throat, omg. What had I done he cared about Julie but didn't want to let his guard down just like Julie wouldn't let her guard down they were both stubborn and it may have just cost them dearly. Mike came flying back into the house as his friend rounded the corner, downstairs the girls were still screaming, the black guy was fucking her and leaned down to grab her hair, Julie scratched his face he was pissed and slapped her so hard her face became to an instant bruise.

Donna seen what happened and started yelling out vulgarities at them the one man grabbed a pillow and put it over her face saying no you wanted this earlier you're getting it now... Mike and the security raced down the steps and saw what was going on. Mike said that's not fun that's being a jackass now get out of my house and take your friends with you. Just about then the security threw a guy across the bar and all the guys gathered up there stuff and was escorted out of the house...

Mike and the guard went back to the girls. Mike went over to Julie and un-cuffed her and brought her to his chest I'm so sorry baby girl I never meant for this to happen. Julie looked up at him by now her eye was black and blue. She smiled at him and said all I ever wanted was for you to love me. I wouldn't have done anything you wanted to make you happy. Mike smiled and said let's get you cleaned up baby. They walked over and saw his friend with a strange look on his face.

Mike said what's wrong he said they must have broken her jaw. I've called an ambulance for her Mike. Julie dropped next to her and started to cry please be ok Donna I can't do this without you. Donna looked into her eyes as tears trickled down her cheeks, and nodded the ambulance got to the house and took her to the hospital. Mike helped

Julie clean up and change and then took her down there, he wanted her checked out anyway and knew if he didn't take her she would never get checked she hated doctors she had been I'll and they were always giving her shots etc. And she swore she would never go again.

When they arrived he asked about Donna, the doctor said she was ok just dislocated her jaw but was resting comfortably right then. Mike turned and brought Julie to him and said would you mind looking at her please she also go hurt there, the doctor said of course take here to room 2.

Mike did they sat and waited for me to come in all while saying I'm fine. I don't even hurt can we just leave. Mike said no baby girl I want you checked then we will go get some dinner and have an early night so we can pick Donna up in the morning ok. Julie smiled and said ok and then it dawned on her you're spending the night. Mike said yes of course I'm not letting you out of my sight again, and when Donna gets home we are going to set a few ground rules if I am going to be staying there.

Julie smiled and said ok sweet, but I'm really ok and I still want to play with you tonight. Mike giggled and said we will see baby girl let's get you something to eat first. The doctor walked back in and asked me to leave the room. Standing up I winked at Julie and left the room walking down to a coffee machine. I need some caffeine. The adrenaline rush was wearing off and I was feeling run down. It had been a long night and I had suspected that asshole was going to be trouble. I should have listened to Julie when she offered to go back upstairs.

That's my life, should haves, and could haves. Shaking my head I looked out the window as Shaun came up. If he hadn't been there it would have gotten very bad for the girls. They going to be alright, he asked. Turning up I nodded yea, Donna has a dislocated jaw and they are checking Julie now. He nodded think you'll have any more trouble out of that guy. Naaaa he's not local. They were from out of town.

The doctor walked out and asked to speak to me. We walked into an empty room and she sat down pointing at a stool. Sitting down my heart felt like it might come out of my chest. I couldn't help but notice that both ladies have been, well sexually active recently. This wasn't a rape was it? A look of relief swept across my face I answered no, no. they are entertainers and things just got out of hand. He looked at me skeptically, ok well I'm going to ask both patients if they want a rape kit done and the authorities notified. Until I get both answers I want you to stay here. I nodded yes sir. He got up and left the room.

Shaun peeked in asking what's up. He noticed their bruises and suspects it might be a rape. You might want to take off in case officers arrive. Shit ok I'll call you tomorrow. Text me if anything comes up/ I nodded and reached out shaking his hand thanks buddy. He turned and left the room and I sat waiting. A few minutes later a nurse poked her head in saying Mike yes ma'am. Doctor said you could come back to room 2 thanks and I got up heading for the room.

Stepping in Julie was slipping the t-shirt back over her head and turned smiling to me. Everything ok. The doctor looked up saying yea she looks fine just some bruising. It should go away in a day or two. I looked back over to Julie and she sat looking worn out, eyes on the floor. You have my number if anything comes up with Donna. The nurse checked yep we've got it she'll be fine. I reach out for Julie's hand taking it and helping her off the table. Can we see her before we leave? Julie asks. Sure the nurse says, right this way I reach shaking the doctors hands thanks for your help and turned to follow Julie and the nurse down the hall. Entering Donna's room she was asleep.

Julie waked up to her bed and bent over kissing her cheek, sweet dreams baby girl. Then turning says we'll better get going baby. I turn and we walk out of the hospital. The drive back to the house was kind of quite. Julie was wiped out and the ecstasy was wearing off leaving her pretty drained. Entering the house she asked would it be ok if we just fixed something here and crashed. I nodded sure, why don't you go take a bath and I'll fix some breakfast. Smiling she moved to me hugging me, thanks for being there for me. I lifted her chin and bent to kiss her. Slowly pulling my lips from hers, where else would I be. She smiles and says, ouch that hurts.

Go on and get cleaned up, breakfast will be ready when you get back down. She turned and said as she was walking away, not too much though I'm not that hungry. I checked through the kitchen, started a fresh pot of coffee and started breakfast. Then I moved into the den and cut on some soft music. A little later I was sipping a cup of coffee when Julie walked back in.

No matter what she looked like, she always looked good to me. Oh gawd I feel so much better now. I laughed saying yea the pain killers they gave you have kicked in huh. She hit me in the arm saying shut up and give me something to eat, then take me upstairs and make me squeal. I pull a chair out for her and she sits down. I pour her a cup of coffee and fix her a plate. Aren't you going to eat? I already have. I turned saying while you eat. I'm going downstairs and clean up a bit. Holler when you are done. She looked up ok but you don't have to do that. I will tomorrow. Naaaa I can do it tonight.

Downstairs the place is a wreck. I straighten the couches out, bag all the trash and take it out. Then I put the bar back together and clean up all the broken glass. It didn't take me to long and I was put back together. It still needed a good cleaning but it was presentable again. I cleaned up the pool table and put the sticks away. Moving to the TV I reached for the video recorder. Don't erase it. I turn to see Julie standing at the bottom of the stairs. Why not because I want to watch the dance Donna and I did. I thought it was pretty good. You sure I ask.

Oh come on Mike. We both know this shit happens. Lucky for me, you and Shaun were here to stop it before it really got ugly. I shrugged. Ok well the rest can wait until another day and walked to her.

What you mean I have you all to myself. She smiled. I grinned looks like baby girl. Julie's eyes widen as she reaches her hand out then come with me sir. I take her hand and we head up the stairs. I cut the lights off as we go up. We keep going and are soon walking into her room. The bed is freshly made and covers thrown back.

Now you go take a shower and I will be waiting she pulled me to her sharing a sweet kiss. I didn't want to let her go. Seemed that I had always been letting her go when all I really wanted was to hold her. Yes ma'am and turned heading for the bathroom. Inside I stripped and now climbed in the hot shower. Gawd it felt good. I was pretty worn out from last night and now tonight.

Seemed the drama never ended. I stood in the shower letting the hot water run over my body. It seemed to draw out all the grief I had felt these last few years.

Stepping out of the shower I couldn't find a towel anywhere. Hey where are your towels come in here I will dry you off. I'm dripping wet. I don't care, come here. I open the door and walk into the bedroom. Julie is sitting on her red Victorian couch in a long white silk robe and holding a towel. Come here sir. Smiling I walked around and stood in front of her. My cock had immediately started to thicken when I saw her and now it was beginning to stand up.

HMMMMMMM. Someone is glad to see me, she jokes as she brought the towel up wiping my chest and arms. Turn around sir. I turn around and she dries my back the down across my ass. HMMMM. I like your ass sir. Shen then dropped the towel further down my legs drying them. Turn please sir. I turn and now my full blown hard cock is in her face. She places the towel over it drying oh sir. I am very glad that I excite you so. Then dropping the towel she reaches around grabbing my ass pulling me to her as she opens her mouth. Slowly taking me between her warm soft lips. Oh gawd I groan as she begins working on me. Gently sucking on the head of my cock and swirling across the head. Gawd she could suck a dick I thought and knew I had to change this or I wouldn't last long.

I pull away and my cock slips from her lips with a pop she is breathing deeply as she sits back looking at me. You've spent the last two nights trying to please me, now let me try and please you. I dropped to my knees before her and tenderly reached for her legs. Her eyes were smoldering as I gently spread her legs. Her robe parted and revealed her pussy to me. She knew what she wanted and she scooted down a little but made sure her robe was under her so she wouldn't mess her couch up.

I slowly began at her knee and start kissing my way up her tight. I was looking up watching her as she opened her robe and done took a tit and began rolling the stiff nipple as the other moved down to softly circle her clit as she watched me. I kissed all the way to her now wet pussy, she held it open wanting me to take it but I quickly kissed her exposed clit bringing oh baby you tease me so good.

Then I started up the other thigh. Now she was pulling on her nipple and thumping her clit as I pushed her hand away and softly kissed it. Her hand reached out to grab my head but I swatted it away and went back to kissing her pussy. Down one side sucking on the lip and back up the other sucking it too. Now both her hands were pulling hard on her nipples gawd baby do it. I lowly run my tongue between her swollen lips and softly OOHHHHHH. Gawd I love how you eat me.

Reaching up I run my hands up he r thighs until I reach her pussy. Then I spread her open and begin running my tongue from her clit to ass. She nearly comes off the couch as my tongue circles her tight asshole. Holy shit Mike. Let me up, please I don't want to mess this couch up. I know she hunted for a while before finding it so, I reluctantly stop and sit back on my heels. Her eyes open and she quickly stands, dropping the robe and moving over to the bed where she crawls up on all fours and raises her ass up. Ok now come do that. Wiggling her ass and spreading her legs.

Smiling I move over onto the bed behind her. Softly blowing across her soaked pussy she mews into the pillows baby gawd please. My tongue slips out and once again between her lips. I can taste her excitement on my tongue now. Reaching up again. I spread her ass open and flick my tongue across her now exposed clit, her body jerks as she cries into her pillow oh yea right there, don't stop.

I circle it a few times and pull back lightly blowing it as I can see it throbbing now, its stiffened out its hood and waiting to set her off. I run my tongue just barely over causing her to scream FUCK, FUCK, and FUCK. It always amazed me how her vocabulary would change so when she was high on ecstasy. I love the way she would cuss and scream. But any other time she was just too inhibited to let it go.

In her mind she was screaming, oh gawd baby, make momma cum, suck my clit. Easing back I trail my tongue along the inside of her thigh and slowly down the crack of her ass. Her body is trembling now as my tongue reaches that tight asshole again. I can feel it began flexing against my tongue as I apply come pressure. My tongue slips through the tight ring and I stroke her ass a couple of times before pulling back and circling it again.

Her hips are bucking each time my tongue gets near her ass. Oh fuck Mike, you that drives me crazy and I plunge my tongue back in her ass. She throws her head back screaming OHHHHHHH GGGGAAWWWWWDDDD, ah she begins soaking me. Her hips are shaking uncontrollably as I hold on, keeping my tongue stroking her puckering asshole.

PLLLLEEEESSSSSSSEEEEE SSSSTTTTTTTTTTTOOOOO OOOOOOPPP!!!!!!! She whined as she couldn't stop cumin. I slipped my tongue free and back down to drink her sweet juices as she collapses on the bed.

Holy fuck Mike you know better than to do that to me. She gasps with a big smile on her face. Rolling over she spreads her legs wide holding her arms out to me come on baby, give momma the fucking she has been waiting for all weekend. I smile and move up between her spread legs. I drag my cock over she clit her hips buck. Shit baby just fuck me please. She reaches down grabbing my cock and holding it at the opening to her soaked pussy, now when we start, don't you fucking dare stop. And then guides me into her very hot pussy.

I groan as I feel the velvety smooth hot envelope engulf me. Leaning forward on my hands. I bend down and kiss her as I slowly begin sliding in and out in long strokes. Her hands reach down and grab my ass setting the pace she wants. She breaks our kiss gasping oh baby only you, and I feel her cumin again. Her pussy was constricting on my cock and her juices running down my balls.

I bend down taking a sweet hard nipple between my lips sucking as she arches he back OH yes, and shows me she wants it a little faster and harder. I follow her lead as she turns back and forth. Feeding me her delicious tits. I was in a zone now. I had watched men enjoy her all night and now I was getting the best prize of all. She seemed to be in a long orgasm as her pussy was still constricting around my cock. Fuck me baby. Give momma what she wants harder. Oh gawd I can't stop she screamed and I fucked her harder and harder. Finally I couldn't last any longer and lifted my head groaning oh shit Julie and shuddered deep in her. Her eyes flicked wide yelling oh baby yes and we both went off together.

I fell against her and she was buried beneath me. Sir roll over please. I'm in a swimming pool down here. I roll of her laughing fuck you are the best baby girl. She is up quick as a cat and attacked me again. She was kissing all over my face and rubbing her super sexed body against mine. You know what it means to me when you call me that and started kissing her way down my stomach.

Reaching my com covered cock, she takes me deep into her mouth cleaning out juices from it. She continues until I'm recovering and she winks at me as I slip from her lips. I knew it wouldn't be long she purred.

Looking up into my eyes. Let's go out to the hot tub for a little while. I could use some hot therapy. I shrug looking over at the clock. It was 11:00. Ok but we need to get some sleep before we go pick Donna up. She nods ok just a little while. I get up and follow her outside.

The night had cooled and it had reverse effects on us. Her nipples got hard as glass and my cock softened. Julie quickly moves into the hot water. Ahhhh. As she slipped in come on you big baby. She teased knowing that it took me forever to get in the hot tub. I began easing myself into it until finally I was in. Damn I thought you would never get here.

She teased as scooted around to sit in my lap. My cock was quickly responding to her attention as she wiggled this way and that way. Mike you know how I feel about you. I nodded yea Julie I feel the same way and I hope you know that. Looking down she continued, I thought I wanted a normal relationship with you but I realize that that's not what I want. If I did have a normal relationship I would be going outside for what I need and I think we both know that. Yea I know that baby girl. She about smothers me with a long very hot kiss. Stop doing that. She teases

So could we have a really, really hot relationship. One where I serve you and you will be my master but one where I can time like that I with you. I look at this incredible woman before me telling me that she wanted a life with me as her master and her lover. I had never considered both. It was always one or the other. How would we separate them I asked, almost talking to myself? Standing up, letting the water run down that incredible body, eyes twinkling, we'll know when to separate them. She stepped out of the hot tub.

Consideration raises from her body like smoke as she stood looking down, I'll be in the play room awaiting you sir and turned walking around the deck.

I watched that sweet ass walk around the corner of the deck. I heard the door open to the play room and the stereo crank up. I could feel my own pulse quickening. How can she do this to me so easily? I'm like a moth drawn to the flame. Slowly standing I step out of the tub and make my way around the deck to stand in the door way of the play room there standing in the center of the room is Julie. She has her head down and wearing her wrist and ankle restraints. How may I please you master.

I don't say a word as I walk in and to her. I slowly circle her contemplating what my pet might enjoy. Smiling I instruct her take of the restraints and wait 10 minutes and then come to your room. Pick up a blindfold a flogger and walk away. She pauses yes sir. Sir do I not please you? I turn and growl do as you were told and walked away.

In her room I strip the wet sheets from the bed. I don't know why because she'll probably soak them if things go well. I slip new sheets on and grab the toilet paper. I then tie a long and short strip to the corners of the bed at the head board. Then I go in the bath room and put some cologne on. Right on time Julie walks into the room. First thing she notices is the bed freshly made and thought is the same as mine why.

Then she notices the toilet paper and her body shudders. Sir I don't know if I can control myself tonight. I look at her you won't disappoint me, will you. Her eyes widen as she looks down no sir. I won't disappoint you. I then hand her the blindfold. As I come close she smells my cologne and presses her body to mine. I want her and she wants me.

I lead her to the bed and help her onto it. She is once again on her hands and knees. I place a pillow beneath her head and chest. I instruct her to spread her hands forward. She does as I instruct and I wrap the tissue around her wrist. Then do the same to her other wrist. Next I spread her legs open and tie the long strips to her knees.

Now any attempt to straighten them the tissue would break. Any attempt to pull her arms back the tissue would break.

Now baby girl I pause and watch as she fights her body not to move if any of your ties are broken then we stop yes sir. I then move away from the bed and let her adjust to her position. Once I feel she is settled I move back forward with the flogger. I drag it across her upturned ass I hear her whimper oh gawd sir. I could her shaking and smiled she was loving it. I had intentionally left slack in all her ties where usually I would have pulled them tight. She had never broken any in the past tests but she had been through a lot tonight so I didn't want it to end with her not completing the task.

I then flipped the flogger across her ass bringing a gasp from her. She raises her head as I begin slow deliberate strokes across her upper thighs with the instrument. I watch and I swear the pussy is so flooded that it's running down her thighs. Oh sir please, please. She pleads as I continue until I see a nice redness appearing. Raise your body I instruct. Carefully so as not to move her hands or knees she raises up on her elbows. As she does I flick the flogger across her hanging tit? OHHHH NO, she pleads as I continue the strikes until her tit is beginning to redden. I then move to the other side of the bed and start on the other one. The tassels of the flogger would flick like a wicked tongue across her swollen nipples. OHHH Sir, I can't she whined but I continued but I continued until tit too was reddening.

I then moved back around and opened her night stand drawer. She couldn't see me but she could hear my every move and I wanted her to. She could smell my cologne and knew where I was and I wanted that. In the drawer found what I was looking for. I t was a bullet vibrator and taking it I turned it on. Her head jerked up when the herd the hum. OH no, please sir.

I picked up a bottle of lube also and then crawled onto the bed behind her. Opening the lube, she heard the click or the cap and dropped her head. Resigned to the fact that this was going to be hard to resist. I poured some lube at the top of her ass crack and watched as it ran down the same path. She was shaking her head no please no.

24

As I reached her sweet asshole, I circled the clinched hole. Teasing it mercilessly. Her head was shaking quickly holy shit sir, you know what that does. I ease the slippery vibe down and around her aching clit. Her hips begin fluttering and I watch her knees and stop before I push her too far. She's gasping now OH I don't if I can sir. Then I push the vibrator against her asshole. Her head shoots up and her body begins rocking against the vibrator. Sir oh gawd sir please. I with drawl the vibrator. And smile patting her ass you are doing very well baby girl.

All movement stops, sir please don't say that.

I move forward and drop my hard cock atop her ass, taking her hips in my hands what, you don't like me calling you my baby girl. I can feel the trimmer run through her body. Smiling I begin stroking my cock through the crack of her ass as I pure more lube down it. She has begun shaking her head again. Sir secure with my wrist and ankle cuffs please she begs what would the fun be of that? I say as I pull back letting the head of my cock run down and over her pulsating asshole and against her waiting pussy.

Do it Sir, take me she growled. Taking the vibrator I again draw it down over her asshole. I knew she thought I was going to slip into her ass while I fucked her but I had something different in mind. Dropping it further down I slipped it deep into her pussy and leaning back pushed the head of my cock against her asshole. OH holy shit, no sir please you can't. Not like this but I pushed harder and soon I had her ass wrapped around the head of my cock and could feel the vibrator in her pussy humming. Her shot up as she screamed.

Oh dear gawd. Release me sir so I can fuck you please.

Gently putting my hands on her hips I just flex my fingers and she does the rest. Soon she is sliding back and forth on my greasy cock. Each slow grind ending with her gasping and pleading. Please sir release my ties. I want to fuck you so bad. I won't answer and keep sliding back and forth. Feeling her ass spasm around my cock. So fucking big Sir. Your dick is driving me crazy. Release me please.

I lean forward across her body and whisper in her ear. If you can endure a little baby girl. Her body began to shake and it was taking all her energy to stay still. I reached around and softly cupped her hanging tits. Oh gawd sir not that. I won't be able to stop. Please release me sir. You know I won't.

My fingers softly run across each big pointy nipple as I continue sliding my cock in and out of her tight ass. I can feel the vibrator deep in her pussy, humming against the thin membrane separating them. Slowly I curl my fingers around each nipple. NO, NO, NO, NO. Sir please release me, I'm so close I can't stop it. Yes you can it's your body. You control it. NOOOOOOOOO Sir, please if you do that I'm going to cum. I slowly close my fingers applying more and more pressure to her sensitive nipples. Her head drops and I can feel he asshole begin fluttering and hear her grunting HHMMMMMMM, as I felt the long squirts spraying across my thighs.

Holding still I will let her go through an intense orgasm leaving her panting. Sir please release me. I reach down and tear the tissue free of her legs and arms saying you did very well baby girl. This set her off again and soon was rocking wildly back and forth on my cock. Oh gawd sir that was so fucking intense. Fuck me. Pinch my nipples sir, harder I continued fucking her until I was close and then I tell her roll over baby girl.

She quickly pulls free of my cock and rolls over spreading he legs wide, I stroke my cock and begin shooting my cum across her body. Her hands reach up smearing the warm cream over her big tits as she purrs gawd sir, I love what you to do me. I fall back on my heels looking at the most erotic scene. Julie laid back, cum covering her big tits and her pussy soaked with her cum.

I fall to her side gasping my gawd you're going to kill me someday. He snuggles up to me saying never Mike, I will never leave you and we drift off into a deep sleep...................

Printed in the United States
By Bookmasters